Love Dummies

Love Dummies

VERA OREN

To order additional copies of this book, contact:
Xlibris
1-888-795-4274
www.Xlibris.com
Orders@Xlibris.com
742405

Contents

To my kids and to my husband who tolerated
my craziness with grace

The older you get, the lonelier you become, and the deeper the love you need.

—Roshi, Zen Buddhist and Leonard Cohen's teacher

1

A STAIN ON THE WINDSHIELD

"Everything is perception, right?" Marta tries to repress her excitement and calm down the kid hiding under her old skin. It is six in the morning, and she is as happy as a tormented teenager skipping school. Today and on any other day from now, she won't have to take the St. Jerome train to work. She retired two months ago. If for a while she was kind of lost, now she is just giddy. She feels like she did in her twenties, when she was ecstatic about life's possibilities that later became destiny. Now she is free, free of love, free of hormones, free of work. Back in the day, she traded her so-called freedom for love—she fell in love, got married, and stayed married even if she had doubts from time to time, doubts brushed away as often as you wipe the kitchen floor after dinner, doubts she believed erupted from a working mom's tired brain. She just didn't pay attention how everything had changed between her and her husband, from whispering to barking, and again to whispering. They loved each other, but life knew how to disintegrate what they had. Even if he had always been a depressed man, loving her in a slightly possessive way with a funny twist, he gave her the most beautiful children on earth, strong enough reasons to stay with him as a trunk committed to the crown of its tree.

She's brewing her morning Lavazza Rosa coffee that smells like joy, looking by the window to check if the white stuff is still covering their lawn. It is an unusually cold day for April, sunny but frisky. This is the time of the year she used to hate because their dogs left black muddy stains, a new form of animal art, on the kitchen's white tiles, which she constantly had to clean. Otherwise, she adored her dogs that are gone now, but that's another story. She was not too sure between taking a dog or a cat and decided to try a cat for a while. Their son's black cat, Sunny, is swirling around her legs. Marta's preparing for the morning ritual, drinking her coffee in the small guest room upstairs, watching the sunrise while checking her e-mails or FB account.

She feels the sunrise is a new show ordered just for her. She sits at her desk looking at the blue sky painted with a pink undertone erupting from behind a few tiny clouds, thin as a nuptial veil, and out of the blue, she sees a myriad of little stars. It's true that everything was an emotional roller coaster before her retirement, but the craziness was followed by a long vacation in St. Thomas. This vacation seemed to slow her down. She cannot be tired. Her sleep is sound now, with no interruption to make imaginary notes about things to be done the next day at the office. Anyhow, her life was easier at work since she changed departments four years ago because, as she said, "If I cannot change my husband, at least I can change my work," a joke, but jokes are most of the time a hidden validation of the truth, a truth afraid to be voiced otherwise.

This morning, she has to finalize her dream trip to the Rockies, the big tour, and her spa appointment, a retirement gift from her brother and her sister-in-law. While doing it, the bright spots in her right eye are replaced by black dots moving into a formation, like an army. She tries to ignore them by flipping through the FB avalanche of postings, looking for Felicia's. Marta doesn't know Felicia personally, but she's read almost all her books published in Canada. Felicia is a respected Romanian writer in Montreal, writing now in English and French. In fact, they almost met twice, but Marta had to leave early to not upset her husband left home alone. Marta loved Felicia's book *Me, Luca and the Chinese*, somehow reminding her of Erika Yong of her youth. She would like to write like Felicia, but for one, she doesn't have her talent, and secondly, her passion is a secret; she cannot mix her crazy thoughts with her social persona.

Today, Felicia posted an article about Ghomeshi, a Toronto media star accused of sexual assault by three women, and commented that she hopes the trial isn't over. Marta looked at the screen and couldn't believe Felicia's comment. This daring lady who wrote *Me, Luca and the Chinese* is buying into the popular opinion about overvictimization of rape victims? Marta finds Ghomeshi's case a disgrace for women, at least for a sixty-year-old like her that knew, when young, how to handle a real sexual assault. Now, the playing field of human courtship is more like a war zone where every date gone wrong could be considered a rape. Many times, men cannot pay a compliment without being considered sexist. It seems that the young women today are lost on a free-for-all game of sex, and because the spectrum of what it is acceptable is so wide, nobody knows the limits anymore. In a society where the new heroes are the LBGTQs, the sex envelope has been pushed so far that everything seems permitted. Somehow it is difficult to grasp the sensitivity of today's women, going from a teenager giving head to her first boyfriend before French kissing him to a mature woman feeling oppressed by a man's gaze.

Marta comments on Felicia's post: "I don't understand what the fuss is about. The three ladies obstructed information, and two of them conspired previously on FB to accuse him. They liked being perceived as victims, but they are not. They were well into their thirties when this happened. How difficult is it to believe that women lie as well? Those ladies chased Ghomeshi as I chased my husband when I was in love with him. I feel offended and ill represented by women taking no responsibility for their *entire* actions." Marta is wondering if her comment will be erased from FB and if Felicia will unfriend her.

By now, the dots in her eyes are followed by a small and fine cobweb. She has no idea what this could be, but Google knows it all. Google decides that she should go to see an ophthalmologist very soon. Instead, she decides to go to the hospital. She opens the garage door where her husband is working and smoking, or working, smoking, and drinking wine even at eleven in the morning.

She says, not too sure about her decision, maybe overreacting again, "Maybe I'm crazy, but I have like a bug in my right eye. I called an ophthalmologist, and he told me to go to the emergency."
He asks, "Can you drive?"

"Yes, for sure, my vision is perfect," she answers.

She knows that he hates hospitals. He suffers from agoraphobia, fly phobia, organic food phobia, cleaning phobia, traffic phobia, standing-in-line phobia, and dishwashing phobia.

She grabs her Kindle, some fruit, some biscotti and a Tupperware with rice and chicken as if preparing for a long flight. She opens the front door. She says bye to Sunny, and off she goes. She starts the engine and looks into the sun. She now sees a mosquito. She closes one eye, and she still sees it. She feels a cold fear like a heavy coat on her shoulders. She only hopes it isn't a brain tumor. Her car passes by their neighbor's house, the one who used to do business with a textile factory in Roman, Romania. He had a brain tumor that killed him in six months.

Driving to Laval hospital takes fifteen minutes on a busy Chomedey boulevard.

She parks her car, enters the emergency, and takes a number. The waiting room is packed. She finds a chair across an old woman with orange hair who is sighing, groaning, coughing, and spitting. On one side sits a businesslike forty-ish woman on high heels incessantly using her iPhone, and on the other side a big and very "tanned"—difficult to describe nowadays the skin color without insulting anybody— young lady accompanied by a man, probably her husband. Marta tries to make eye contact with the tanned lady to apologize as she feels her unease when, for a split of second, Marta's hand is too close to hers.

Today Marta was supposed to babysit, and she won't be able to. Now it's 1:00 PM, and she should pick up her granddaughter Cloe from *garderie* in Laval at 5:00 PM. She opens the me-machine, or her cell, to send a warning SMS to her daughter Lisa: "I'm at the emergency. I have a bug in my eye since this morning. No babysitting today." followed by three emojis crying, thinking that Cloe, now only three years old, will soon write SMS using only emojis.

Her cell starts chirping, but she is called to triage where two young nurses ask the usual questions, take her blood pressure, the temperature, and do a quick eye exam. She's classified as a mild emergency, but the mosquito in her eye does not want to go away.

When out of triage, she sends another SMS to her best friend Ella: "Baby, I'm having an adventure at the emergency, and I am scared. I have a bug in my eye."

Lisa's SMSs starts poking: "Did you fall last night at tennis? Are you dizzy? Can you see properly?"

"No. No. Yes. I feel fine," Marta answers in spite of the fact that she experienced a slight vertigo just before entering the emergency.

"Did they do a proper eye exam?"

"Not yet."

Every fifteen minutes or so, Lisa's or Ella's SMS would blink at her asking for news. Ella was spreading the news in their group and informs Marta that two other friends have had something similar for some years now and that it is nothing to worry about.

In spite of Ella's news, Marta could not concentrate enough to read her Kindle. Moving her butt from one painful heap to another, Marta is imagining how people around her see her. She has doubts that she looks good for her age, even if her friends tell her that. Her inner age is maybe thirty, but her flesh and bones are sixty. She remembers her grandmother, a lively spirit hidden under a black long dress, a grey apron, and a colorful *basma* patterned with red roses. "What is natural is beautiful and impossible to explain." Her grandmother used to say many things that didn't make sense to Marta, but nevertheless, she absorbed them with hunger. Marta is grateful to be a woman in this century. She compares herself with her grandmother and can appreciate the change.

Marta's generation had it all, the first women penetrating men's workfields, in her case computers, marrying for love, enjoying having kids, family, and a job, sometimes tricky to handle, having fun at work, and flirting without feeling assaulted by men's compliments. Marta sees herself as a responsible, tough, and confident woman. She is not prudish as many of her Romanian friends are, and she can appreciate a vulgar joke without feeling offended. She experienced unpleasant moments in the past, but she learned how to neutralize a man who went too far.

In retrospect, she is proud of how she handled her boss's sexual harassment in the '90s, the Anita Hill period. She was working in Varennes, in the far east of Montreal, and commuting every day from Kirkland, the far west of Montreal, crossing the city, taking the 40 up to the Lafontaine tunnel and continuing on the 132 Est. She used to leave home at 6:00 AM. Getting back to the West Island by 6:00 PM to pick up the kids after school from *service de garde* was very often a challenge. Many times, during winter she was not able to make it. Peter Dunkl, at the time in charge of the Service Center at the same corporation, knew her life was not easy. He created a marketing job in the West Island office and offered it to her. She jumped on it, considering him a savior. It was too good to be true. It was a trap. At the time, she was thirty-five with two toddlers in tow while Peter Dunkl was sixty, no kids, and a terminally ill wife.

"Poor guy, I am his only joy!" Marta used to think while being constantly verbally harassed and expecting the worst. She did her best to avoid him while looking for another job. She didn't talk to anybody, except her husband, and she had to face the real music every day for one year, scared that she could lose a job she needed.

That is why Ghomeshi's main accuser is a disgrace in Marta's eyes. Marta can picture Dimanno at the Christmas party where everything started, high heels, well dressed, provocative, and assertive, no babies crying at home, a perfect night for having fun.

Don't tell me she doesn't know how to handle a man. Come on! For this lady, Ghomeshi was a challenge. Otherwise, why did she stalk him after being choked? Those women are acting as if they don't have sexual impulses, only the men. Ladies, wake up! Are you willing to have a society with castrated men? Because you are heading this way! Your husbands are doing much more than our husbands ever did, cleaning, cooking, and spending time with the kids. What do you expect? To drug your man to get hard only when you feel like it? Would you like a man without a gaze of desire? But this gaze is natural. It's part of the game of courtship.

Marta is fuming when she thinks of young women wearing miniskirts at minus twenty degrees Celsius still pretending this makes them feel good about themselves—she, for one, would feel cold, really cold—or "going out with the girls" and drinking shooter after shooter.

Those young ladies don't look prudish to Marta. They look unleashed. Besides, every girl at puberty is shortening her long high school skirt to show off her legs without being programmed by men, but by hormones. Why then do those ladies feel that they're oppressed by men looking at them and that they're manipulated by fashion, an industry invented by men, even if most of the fashion designers are proudly gay?

Let's blame the man, in spite of biology, in spite of the fact that all of us, boys and girls, are curious, even fascinated by our sexual identity since we can remember.

According to Marta, the intention of the act of love is about solitude and surrender, without witnesses, and nobody can ever judge what happened between the two as nobody can guess a couple's harmony by the way they act in society. Nobody knows what happens when they are alone, naked, vulnerable, themselves. The act of love is natural and magical, impossible to define and desiccate. It is a search for a gentle touch, many times initiated by despair or soul searching, an act that can easily switch from tenderness to neo-feminist a *rape* definition when the magic is broken by a gesture, by a whisper, by a scream.

Rape has two heads and both are ugly. The media is invaded by rape reports, the rate being higher now because single young women feel less ashamed. However, no wife in her right mind talks about the rape in the conjugal bed, the worst rape of all, the quiet and slow soul killer.

Marta looks at the women still sitting by her side. The one to her left could very well be a Ghomeshi's accuser. She is elegant and looks independent. The Arabic woman sitting to her right is not speaking any language except Arabic and has to be accompanied by her man to communicate with the world around her. You can see she is angry and wounded on the inside.

Why can't the woman to my left see how the woman to my right is suffering? How come she is so selfish? Why don't those New Age Amazonians engage in the real war against the Muslim traditionalists who treat women like convicts? Or this is too tall of a call for some rich and entitled brats? The Canadian-born woman is disgusted by the gaze of a man but not by an honour crime against a veiled woman who wants to be free to choose her man.

Marta finds the New Age Amazonians hysterical. They seem empty inside. They are hungry for love but blinded by their hate. They are not accepting their own nature; they are fighting themselves. They are feminists, but not feminine anymore. They are tough without being compassionate. They are sexual, without being sensual.

She hears her name. She's being called to room no. 5. She enters the room dedicated to the eye exam. The doctor is a young and efficient woman. The eye exam, unpleasant because of all the multicolored liquids poured into her eyes, is over in ten minutes. Her eyes look okay, but the young doctor has to check her heart and her brain. It takes only two hours to complete all the tests, even the brain scan. Soon after, she is parked among stroke victims, in zone B of the emergency ward, where she is waiting for her results. Her bed is just in the middle of the hallway, and on each side she sees four well-equipped partitions. The patients in the partitions are much older than her, or so she likes to think. She feels good that she didn't get a bed in a partition; this means she will be home in no time.

Meanwhile, her daughter, her best friend, and now her son too, are burning her cell battery sending SMSs asking for news. From her location, as within the eye of the tornado, she can enjoy the show of young and colorful male nurses dressed in flowery uniforms coming and going constantly, taking blood pressure, and temperature. Another society flip, a society where women are doctors and men are nurses. Most probably, those assertive women doctors are craving to have babies, still alone at thirty-five, and looking for a macho sperm donor. This is the new society where procreation became a manufactured, controlled process without a soul. Even looking into someone's eye is a challenge; nobody has the time anymore because their eyes are glued to me-machine.

Her neighbors, the two ladies from the waiting room, are also here, dressed to kill in their hospital gowns with butterflies imprints. They are all suddenly equal, stripped from our customs, our veils or our miniskirts, naked, exposed, afraid, waiting for the verdict.

Zone B is full. On one side, the Arabic lady is in pain now and unable to explain anything without her man, and two old women, one eighty-five, waiting for a diagnosis for two days and by now indifferent that her gown is open in the back for maximum comfort, the other ninety, coming straight from a bingo game where she had a seizure. On the other side are three angry men, one very fit and old, complaining that he lost all his friends, one younger who just came back from Florida to see his grandson's hockey juniors final, and the third, a survivor of a major stroke thirty years ago, ready to tell the story of how lucky he was to survive the stroke. To make things simpler, most of the old patients, when asked, chose to wear diapers for the night.

Every two hours, a black male nurse from Cote d'Ivoire—she knew that tiny detail about him because she heard his conversation with another black nurse about a YouTube video from Cote d'Ivoire that makes fun of the terrorists (a good one indeed!)—passes to check on them. When Marta asks if she has to stay the night, his answer is always the same: "Fifty-fifty chances." What the hell does this mean?

In order to calm down, hoping not to have a brain tumor, Marta starts shuffling through her e-mails, 90 percent hidden spam. Her Yahoo account is for light communication, high school, work colleagues, or distant friends. She has three other Gmail accounts, one for her writing, one for her regular work, and one for her family and close friends.

She's lucky to find a fresh e-mail with Romanian jokes she hadn't yet read. Going through it, she starts smiling, and by the fourth joke, she is laughing her head off. It is 1:00 AM. Her neighbors look intrigued at first. The two old women start contagiously laughing. The Arabic woman looks offended while the men look really angry, disturbed by her laugh, their sleep too thin.

"It has been finally proven that men can concentrate on two things at the same time, the boobs."

"Why is a man always ready to go to bed with a new woman, but he's afraid to get viruses from an USB borrowed by a friend?"

"Why do doctors speak Latin? To help their patients to get used to a dead language."

Marta is looking around. Nobody has a sense of humor anymore except old women. She decides not to create a stir in the ward and tries to go to sleep, but it is impossible. She is constantly brushed by running nurses, absorbed doctors, and late family visitors. She feels like she is in the middle of a highway. When, for a moment the ward is quiet, she feels like a convict during an interrogation, a light blinding her and crushing her brain with a heavy aura. She usually sleeps turned onto her left side but now her left arm has a needle in it, the ultimate torture.

At four or five in the morning, she is startled by a scream. She opens her eyes to see the major stroke survivor screaming, his exposed butt literally in her face. "I need water and a new diaper!" This is a reminder that she's been here for almost twenty-four hours, and she hasn't drank any water. She also asks, embarrassed somehow, for some water. The young black male nurse brings water only for her, and the grumpy old man starts screaming again, "You like her more than me? I was the first one asking for water!"

She feels even worse half an hour later when the doctor who releases her tells her she would need an ophthalmologist eye exam a month later, just for the follow-up.

She takes her purse and leaves, knowing she has to get used to seeing life through a stain on her windshield.

2

THE YELLOW DRESS

It was the second Saturday of September 1975. The streets were dusty. The sky decided to stay naked, its heavy blue falling on the leaves of the linden trees. No clouds for more than a week. The sun was sucking the green out of the leaves, leaving behind red spots of unwashed blood. The poplars, skinnier and greyer than last year, were like soldiers fighting the low-rise buildings in this Bucharest's neighborhood, their trunks wet from the stray dogs' peeing. The same dogs were barking all night long, giving nightmares to her little sister, Maya, whom she shared the bedroom with.

Adriana came back a few days ago from Piatra Neamt after staying with her aunt during the summer. She has the same strange feeling as she has each summer, after a three-month vacation, that well-known objects are bigger or inflated as if the air is lighter in Bucharest. This fall, she is starting university. She is now a student in engineering, a choice she made in spite of her family wish to go into medicine. In fact, her real wish was literature, but she chose science as a comfortable and practical compromise.

That night was the freshmen's ball, and the coming Monday would be the first day of her freshman year. She was excited. Since being back in Bucharest, Adriana's parents granted her a freedom she didn't know what to make of. She was not used to it. Her parents kept her away from bad influences because in Romania danger was everywhere; they refrained from discussing politics at home even if Adriana's father was persecuted by the regime. She knew because she had found in a drawer, underneath his handkerchiefs ironed by her mom, secret letters and petitions sent by her father asking for his old position as a teacher. Adriana was hardly able to read, but she was not shocked. She accepted the verdict as a destiny, the destiny of people who were rich before the Communists came to power. Adriana adored her father, a skinny and tall man with grey eyes, and she craved for his love and attention. But her father kept a distance, hugging her rarely, his sad face illuminating when she was coming home from school with a 10 or even with the best student crown. She always wanted to please her farther, to see this glow of pride on his face! There were rare the occasions when he used to take her by her shoulders to get her close to his lanky body and squeeze her tight.

Adriana's father was the supreme judge in their house, a gentle judge, but Adriana felt betrayed three times The first time was when she was in the first grade, she got a homework on calligraphy, handwriting being an art back then. Her father was drunk, and he ripped her homework ten times(this was the first and the last time they ever did homework together). The second time was in the second grade when one night when she came home from the park in front of their block where she was playing with her friends, she found her mom alone on her knees in the middle of the family room crying over their wedding pictures, and the third time was when her father started sending her to bed one hour earlier every Tuesday to keep her from listening to Europa Libera.

Adriana's mom was the messenger and the executor. She was like an albatross flying around her head, following Adriana everywhere to protect her from the regime, from her crazy girlfriends, or from sexually obsessed boys or men. When Adriana was fourteen, while spending her summer vacation at her grandma's in the village, she exchanged subversive letters with Manuela, her best friend, who was at Mamaia on Black Sea shore. Who knew that even the inside Romania, letters could be intercepted? When back to school in the fall, both girls and their parents were reprimanded in the school's director office.

Adriana had a happy childhood. It was the '60s in Romania. The shops were not empty yet, and the park where she played with other kids was well maintained. They were a gang of twenty or so kids getting together in the park surrounded by the four-floor buildings. They were playing hide and seek, *hotii si vardisti* and *poarca*. When the kids grew up, some of them paired up into couples. Then the boys became a danger in her mother's eyes, the family rules became stricter, and Adriana had to lie constantly to go to a *ceai* that usually was starting at 3:00 PM where the host's parents were gone for a day to visit relatives outside Bucharest. Her mom used to see enemies everywhere, boys that put pills in girls' drinks to assault them. But Adriana didn't pay attention. She knew she could spot a dangerous man. Many times, she experienced encounters with men showing their dicks in the park or pressing their bodies against hers in a crowded tramway. She knew how they looked. She was not afraid, and she could deal with them.

Adriana was a dreamer in a society where brainwashing was a must. She was blind to any information except the Communist propaganda, buying what the newspapers were selling, refusing to know more. She was drunk with beautiful ideals, in love with the "Freedom for Palestinian People" and wearing an Angela Davis pin badge. She was looking for a cause to dedicate herself to, but she didn't have enough imagination or courage. *Faute de mieux,* she embraced the hippie movement, Romanian brand because it was easy to fight against black slavery, and not against the Communist slavery. She liked American music because the boys she liked loved it, but she never understood the words of those songs. She was uplifted by others' ideals that became hers. She was an avid literature reader, from Proust, Kafka, Sadoveanu, Rebreanu to Eugen Barbu and Augustin Buzura. She read everything, nothing else to do during summers.

She started her day as usual with a Turkish coffee, a Romanian tradition since the Ottoman rule, secretly craving for a cigarette while looking out the bedroom window of their apartment, too small for a family of four and their bulky and shiny furniture. At least, her mom didn't expose the gypsy's painting that you could see in every Romanian house, a beautiful gypsy girl wearing an *ia* and showing a naked boob. Adriana never understood the Romanians' obsession with the gypsy painting as if to outnumber Ceausescu's portraits adorning every meeting room or classroom. Adriana decided that tonight she would be going alone to the ball alone. None of her friends were in engineering. That night she would be a risk taker.

Two days ago, she strolled through downtown Bucharest to buy a new dress and a pair of sandals for her big entrance into this new chapter of her life. She did it with her best friend, Elisa, who failed her admission exam to ASE (economics) and had to wait for next year to try again. Elisa was a beauty, Adriana not so much. They were the perfect match for the Romanian saying "Mom had two daughters. The gorgeous one went to ASE, the other one to engineering."

Adriana would never buy anything from Eva or from Victoria shops, too tacky. She likes *Fondul plastic* on Magheru Victoria Boulevard, but there everything was too expensive for her parents' budget. Instead, she went to Romartizana on Victoria Boulevard and bought a yellow transparent mini dress. She loved the fine melted linen inspired from the embroidered Romanian peasant blouse, a blouse popular even among the hippie movement, worn without a bra as the gypsy in the picture. Her dress, yellow as a duckling just dried up from his egg house, was far from being virginal. She would have liked a black dress, more her style, but there was no choice of color. She matched her dress with a pair of yellow sandals, heavy, like an army boot on high platforms. With a mini dress and high platforms, her long legs looked even longer. She hated wearing a bra, and not wearing one was another kind of rebellion. Anyway she had no money left for a nice bra. Besides, the bra was not part of the hippie movement! Make love, not war!

The ball started at 6:00 PM. When she left at 7:00 PM, she disregarded her mom's look that seemed to scream, "My daughter is naked!" She lied that before going to the ball, she will meet with Eva Fisher, her colleague from high school.

She got to the main building on top of Grozavesti hill after taking the tramway all the way across the city. Inside the hall, the music was loud, but the place almost empty. She was kind of hoping to meet Eva Fisher there, but Eva was too high on the social ladder, too beautiful and popular to come to such an event. Eva already had a boyfriend and planning to immigrate to the USA.

Adriana noticed a guy she had met during the admission exams. She was intimidated by his appearance, tall with a moustache and the demeanor of an outlaw, but she had no other choice. In the same group, there were three others guys, all of them smoking. The "outlaw" guy made space for her in their circle without engaging in anything similar to an introduction. One of the four, skinny with long hair and a distant look, was the only one who shook her hand and whispered his name, Radu. It was obvious he was there against his will, and he would rather do something else. He was sitting like a bird on a wire, on a steel rail protecting the windows, detached and superior, exuding mystery. She noticed his tight pants with bell bottoms as large as his big foot, made of heavy canvas. He was explaining to a chubby guy how he should have played a bridge hand last night at the dorms. The fourth one had a familiar face. Adriana vaguely remembered this slim boy with dark skin and curly black hair, looking like a basketball player, being in her class during the exams. The dark-skinned boy's name was Cristian, and he was the only one approachable. Adriana and Cristian chatted for a while, and they danced together on a Demis Roussos song, trying to do what they came here for. They stopped after two songs because both agreed that the music was awful. The fat guy, Alex, was constantly speaking, making funny remarks about anybody passing by, especially girls. Adriana was embarrassed, but she couldn't stop laughing.

Then a boyish man with dark hair and skin, looking confused, came straight to their group, making an effort to smile. Before he started chatting in broken Romanian, Adriana overheard the fat boy whispering with an undertone of sarcasm, "He is Palestinian, and he will be studying with us."

Maybe the Palestinian overheard what the fat boy said, and that's why he asked Adriana to dance. She refused him, mainly because the huge platforms made him shorter than she was. Adriana saw something exotic and strange in this man maybe because it was her first time meeting a foreigner. The newcomer had to stay and do nothing while awkwardly looking for something in the back pockets of his jeans. He was the only one wearing jeans. The disco music was louder and louder.

Finally, Adriana understood that this evening was going nowhere, and she decided to go back home—the future could wait another day! But the Palestinian decided to come with her to the tram station.

"The music was horrible. Mine is much better," he said on the way out while he was opening the door for her.

"Yes, you are right. I don't like disco music. I love the Beatles," she said.

"If you like, we can try 333, a disco place not far from here, but if you want to listen to some Beatles, come to my dorm. Nobody is there now, and you can enter the boys' dorm without any problem," he proposed.

Adriana is trying hard to remember what happened, what made her accept the invitation and what had been said during the long walk from the ball hall to his dorm. Her memory is shredded like an old lace. She doesn't even remember his name, and she didn't like him. She only remembers that it was a warm night. Maybe she felt awkward because of the fat boy's comments. Maybe she felt empathy for a refugee. Maybe she imagined the Palestinian's family displaced. Maybe she was a real Communist trying to balance the injustice done by Israel.

They went to the second dorm of the complex aligned along the Dimbovita River. His dorm, like a cube from an overly used wooden puzzle game with the paper pictures peeled off, had a greyish hue lined with "Fuck" or "Suck my dick" and other popular and obsessive boys' curses. She was not appalled even if they was worse than any student's funny songs. Nobody cared to keep the dorms or the parks in shape. The grass was not cut, but the trees still had the skirts of white chalk. At least, the white tree skirts were illuminating the night and helping them to see the dorm's entry better. Once inside, the dark was shyly lit by a timid forty-watt light bulb, and she felt a bit like in Orwell's *1984*, a book she didn't finish yet.

They stopped at the second floor. Seeing the long dark hall, she had a hesitation. For a second, she felt as in a prison where the inmates were conspiring against her. The floor was too silent as if all the rooms were deserted. He explained, "This is the dorm for foreign students, and many of them haven't arrived yet from their countries."

Angela Davis spoke to her in thought, *What segregation!*

The room was a single room, a luxury in Romania, a desk, a closet, and a bed. She was surprised; usually the rooms are for two or three students. Right there, you could see a little sign of what money can do. She didn't know yet that the foreign students had a special status only because of the power of the green, Romania being fascinated by the dollar. She didn't know yet that those students were part of the upper class in Romania, equal only to Communist party members, a foreigner being able to buy exams, meat, friendship or love, Kent cigarettes, chewing gum, or sheer stockings with U.S. dollars while a high-ranking apparatchik was able to buy everything with a wink or a vague promise of protection.

He showed her his collection of vinyl LPs, and she chose an old Beatles *Sergeant Pepper's Lonely Hearts Club Band.* She heard from a friend some years ago that it was a good one. He recommended Abba instead, a name she hadn't heard yet. He offered a cognac, but she preferred beer. He had some Tuborg beer cans in his new fridge, another sign of prosperity.

"Do you want to dance?" he asked. She found this strange; she only wanted to listen to the music. He convinced her to listen to ABBA, those two high-pitched ladies' voices. She agreed but didn't know how to dance here alone with him in an empty room. Besides, by now she was positive that he was much older than her, and he was following a well-written scenario. She didn't like him at all. A slow song came after the disco music of ABBA, and he got closer to her, pushing his torso against her breasts. She looked in his eyes, and she had a strange feeling that she can see there the nightmarish vision she had when she was three year old and her grandparents were slaughtering their rosy pig for Christmas. A bitter taste like the tannin of a strong dark red wine invaded her mouth, and the wine of fear turned her body soft.

The empty walls were reverberating the music. His mouth, too close to hers, gave away the sweet and heavy smell of vomit. The music was lingering on her skin as a cold salamander, and the light seemed to her too bright, blinding all her senses, her bones made of wax. She was confused, suddenly realizing she was in danger. In a split second, the same soft body became tense and ready to run as a jungle prey. She was light like a feather but sweating like a horse after a race.

She pushed him away from her gently, but he got closer instead, pressing himself against her while whispering in her ear in a rough Romanian with a heavy accent, "Let's not play games!"

She looked at him. "I don't play games, and I want to leave now. NOW! I have to catch my tramway."

He checked his watch replying, "It's not even 10:00 PM. We still have time." And at the same time, he locked the door and put the keys in his jeans. Then she noticed under his desk a carton box opened and full of jeans.

He laughed. "You are my prisoner, my little yellow duckling!" he said with a stronger accent, not caring anymore to speak a clean and acceptable Romanian.

She was not terrified anymore because she had to put her energy into escaping. She knew what he wanted, and she also knew he will never get it from her. She was ready for the challenge, and she was ready for the fight.

He was getting close again trying to assess the situation by the expression on her face. She was able to see herself in the convex of his dilated irises as in a distorted mirror. She was taller than him because of the sandals. She also knew she could use them as weapons, their platforms heavy enough to hurt a strong man. Her senses were on edge. She was able to feel the sound of dead leaves falling down on the pavement of the dorm entrance.

With her on high platforms and her short dress, he had no problem reaching between her thighs and touching her crotch with a hand made of steel. Afraid that he will rip off her underwear and she will have nothing to wear, she just took them off, teasing him at the same time and hoping she could reach for his key in his front pocket while his excitement grew. Her neurons were shooting information to one another at lightspeed, trying to find solutions to startle this man without a name.

He was taken aback, but he attacked her again with his hands. To make it less handy for him to fondle her standing, she took off her sandals and made a clearer picture of their position, not too far from the bed.

He whispered, titillated, "My duckling is cooperating! Nice move!" He was trying to make an opening between her legs with his left leg as if dancing a passionate tango. The tango continued during two other disco ABBA songs, and still he was not able to open her legs. She had good, strong legs. He tried kissing her, but she was turning her head around as if a mechanical toy, laughing at the same time. While he was gasping for air looking for a place to kiss her, she grew more confident, smelling and touching his frustration. To stop her from moving, he opened her arms, immobilizing her against the wall in a crucifix position and finally kissing her neck. She started screaming, but her voice was muffled by his mouth for a second or two, her scream sounding like an echo underwater or a scream of pleasure. She was unable to reach his pocket to find the key. Her hands were tied.

"You scream for nothing. Everybody is at the ball," he said victorious.

She lost her cool for a minute. He felt it in his gut, and he pushed her on the bed. In the fall, her short and loose dress flew over her tummy to show him her intimacy. She saw the change in his eyes, going from a wolf's to a lion's, transforming his features. Even his hair became a crown, a black crown.

The fight continued in the bed, she trying to find the key while he was undressing her with expert moves, their bodies entwined, looking like a monster or a huge bug. She heard the key falling under the bed together with his jeans. His victory made her stronger. He attempted to penetrate her, but her feminine flower was completely closed, impenetrable. This made him roar like an animal, not accepting the obvious. Not letting him be tender with her, she increased her chances to stay closed, no key to her opening to be found. He had only one solution, to push and try to penetrate her by force and fatigue. It didn't happen. After two hours of intense unfulfilling sex, he just gave up while he was still hard but tired of fighting for every millimeter.

Adriana doesn't remember if he let her freely or if he pushed her out the door or how she recovered her panties and her sandals. She remembers only her long walk home on the empty streets of Bucharest, from Grozavesti to her neighborhood, a yellow duck crawling home, her pride shredded. She had to sit on the boardwalk for a moment to recollect. She cried for a while, a mute and soft cry, a lost duckling without her mom. When she stood up, she felt a wave of heat between her thighs as the first rosy drops of virginal blood were cleaning the last trace of a man inside her.

When finally home, just before entering the building, she was surprised that not a single stray dog barked at her, maybe out of respect. Maybe she was an alpha female, a broken one now, her muscles aching from the heavy fight. She knew her parents were not sleeping when she arrived home around 2:00 AM even if they didn't move or sigh. Her sister was sound asleep in their common bedroom.

She went to bed exhausted, knowing that tomorrow she won't be a virgin anymore. Tonight, she had been initiated. She played Tarots cards with herself. At least, she found out how stupid and brave she could be. She never blamed the offender. She blamed herself, the enabler. Since that night, she became splendid at forgetting, lying to herself and everybody else. The next morning, she decided, as a well-trained warrior, she doesn't want a family.

Walking on Diamond beach in Martinique, Adriana feels an old visceral fear, a fear she believes dissolved in the cleaning fluid of her brain and forgotten for forty years. She stops to look at her feet in the water, layers and layers of blue pleats with white lace, washing her soaring ankles. In the light of dawn, the lace looks, for a split of a second, as a yellow dress shredded to pieces, an obscene lace, a human pollution, washed away by the sea.

Adriana is an early bird and a free spirit, how free or crazy some New Age BS can get you to, as Radu, her husband of thirty-five years, says. Radu is still sleeping, and she envies him for that. It seems that with age, he is sleeping more, and she is sleeping less. She doesn't complain. Her mornings alone are a good preparation for the day. This year, they wanted to spend a long vacation alone, no kids, no friends, as a trial for their retirement. "Let's see if we can be alone together" as Leonard Cohen taught them.

After so many years, she has doubts about the yellow-dress episode. She doesn't remember much as if a fog is covering everything for witnesses' protection. Everything was done in silence, the worst scream of all. The man in her memory has no face. The girl in the yellow dress is a fool.

3

ISRAEL IS EVERYWHERE

Anda came to me in my sleep at dawn while I was dreaming I was flying. She whispered, "I trust you, Auntie." She had the Canadian flag in her hands. I lost the balance of my invisible wings and fell in a pool of murky water. I couldn't open my eyes, half underwater half under white foam. Anda's story has been bubbling inside me for some time. Stories always grow in my head in the twilight zone between dreams and reality, and even if my imaginary pen is dry, the stories make me toss in my bed till I get up and go straight to my desk. Some stories I resist for years, but I always end up writing them. Some stories come to me naturally, like a waterfall. I wake up, and poof, they are waiting for me on the keyboard.

I resisted Anda's story for a long time, hoping for it to go away, hoping not to become a story. I am writing it now, but I am not happy with how I started. I would like to keep the wings I had in my dream and fly to Anda's nest in the core of Tel Aviv. She is a Jew who is afraid to live in Israel. The same place was full of beginnings for me, a *shiska*. I was her age when I stepped on Israel's land, a land I never considered holy. I loved Israel and I was neither Jewish nor a tourist. I spent my youth and my love there. Israel was my first encounter with a real democracy after spending the first twenty-five years of my life under a communist regime. Anda made me laugh once: "Israel is like a beautiful lady everybody wants to fuck, and because they never succeed, they are denigrating her."

Now, after thirty years in Canada, from my bed placed in a feng shui way in order to face south in a bedroom painted white and blue and too big for one person, in an old house with white aluminum sidings, on a quiet street unpaved and full of potholes, in a suburb of Montreal, I see Israel as the safest place on earth. But as Leonard Cohen says, "I don't trust my inner feelings / inner feelings come and go."

I am awake now. It's late for me, already 7:00 AM. Today is Canada Day and, for a change or because of climate change, it is sunny outside. I am starting my laptop kept on my night table ready to type crazy ideas coming to me when I am not fully awake. The computer screen freezes my mind and stabs my flesh. Horror again! My fingers are numb on the keyboard. Panic struck me, the same panic that used to struck my guts and my bones thirty years ago when *Mabat* reporters were barking war news or dead Israelis soldier names. *Hadashot*, the news at 9:00 PM, were watched religiously by the entire nation, the air in every house in Israel vibrating with fear.

This is Montreal! Why am I afraid? After Brussels, Paris, Orlando, Istanbul, today twenty Westerners were killed by ISIS sympathizers in Bangladesh. Whose turn next? Which street in which city will be flooded by candles and flowers and ribbons and people crying and hugging? Which TV station will run the same horrific videos ad nauseam? Which uninspired anchorman will ask the same silly question to a random witness: "How did you feel when you saw people dying in front of you?" Apocalypse is right before my eyes sharing the screen with the news of Elie Wiesel's passing as if my hero couldn't stand today's dementia and preferred to cross the dark river to the realm of the infinite silence.

We left Israel in 1984 because we didn't agree with the Likud's politics. We left Israel a year before Anda was born and the Intifada started, choosing a safer place and settling down in Montreal. Why do I now feel that the Israel I knew is everywhere, no way to escape a globalized Intifada turning into inferno? But this story is not about me. It is about Anda.

I close my eyes. I feel safer when not facing the reality. I am again half human, half bird flying over borders, hate and despair. I am crossing the Atlantic Ocean, pass Gibraltar, continuing over the Mediterranean Sea, entering the flourishing strip of land that many call Haaretz without even knowing Hebrew. I am flying over Tel Aviv beach, wing to wing with seagulls and cormorants, my body light. This is a place where I want to be, noisy, hot, a beach at noon. I am looking for Anda. She is twenty-five today.

If you, occasional reader, have enough time to spare when visiting Israel—obviously you are visiting for religious reasons—you should know that you are there for the wrong reasons. You better go to Tel Aviv beach to know what Israel is really like. You should start walking on the Tel Aviv beach at the yacht club and head south to Yaffo, the Tel Aviv's ancestor, a historical jewel but also the place for too many terrorist events. This way, you can have a micro-Israeli experience. Up north, in front of Dan Hotel, you can see the rich Americans tanning or elegant ladies with white pearls walking their hysterical dogs on the beach. If the afternoon heat of July hasn't kill you yet, your path will cross young students of all possible skin colors, most of them with curly hair and Semitic noses, playing a version of beach ping-pong, an Israeli game named *matkot*, splashing water when jumping to get the ball. Loud music is playing, interrupted from time to time by screams and greetings, "*Hacol beseder, Habibi*" or "*Yala, hevre.*"

The Tel Aviv beach is not a quiet place, nor is it polite. Nobody in Israel will make space for you to pass even if you say, "*Sliha.*" Bumping into people is normal. It is crowded and everybody is on the edge, no time for formalities. Israelis are educated to be irreverent and never bend their knees. When the Arabs declared they would kill and throw all the Jews into the sea, the Jews believed it. After World War II, everybody in Israel takes seriously any threat. If you pass the hotels, you get to the beach restaurants aligned along Hahoff Street where you can drink a cold Maccabi beer with a Greek salad à la *isrealienne* sitting at a table with your feet in the hot sand. Here, along the elevated street, a *taielet* winding down till Yaffo as a serpent with scales made from the same white rosy cobblestone as all of Yaffo buildings, you won't see any Orthodox Jews. They are considered mere troublemakers or social parasites by the vast majority of Israelis but tolerated as long as they cannot get a majority in the Knesset.

It's obvious I love Israel, no? I might be biased. I love Israelis and their *hutzpa*. As a Romanian shiska, by default, I am modest and lenient, leading my life according to an old Romanian saying, "A bent neck is an insurance against beheading." This have been a must during the Ottoman rule. That's why I am admiring the young Israelis for being arrogant, proud, and determined to fight after they mourned their grandparents, uncles, and aunts slaughtered like sheep during the Holocaust. The young Israelis' irreverence is the antipode to the Holocaust survivors' resilience suffering in silence, embracing life with a heart of gold, trying to forget. Holocaust survivors never went back to Germany to kill the Nazis' grandkids for revenge.

Israel is also a melting pot of all complexions and cultures, from the dark Ethiopians to the ginger, freckled Russians, and from the upper-class snobbish French art collectors to the poor Jewish coming from a desert in Morocco. Israel is born from despair and hate and flourished with love, hope, and determination, thriving like a sunflower fed from Birkenau and Auschwitz ashes.

When you get really exhausted and you can see clearly the minaret of the Yaffo mosque with the four round roofs as blue as the sky, or when you can hear the city's humming fading away and the beach is quiet, you know that you are close to Shuck Hacarmel, the Oriental core of Tel Aviv and secular Israel, as the Wailing Wall is the core of religious Israel. Shuk Hacarmel is a micro image of Israel, a circus of Mizrahi music, multicolored vegetables and fruits, cheap fabrics and beachware with vendors constantly screaming, all mixed with a heavy air of fried falafel. You can leave the beach behind you, cross the busy Hahoff Street, and instead of going straight, you can turn right to enter Kerem Hateimanim, an old and decrepit corner of Tel Aviv now invaded by artists, a place where Israelis are not burdened by history as they are when strolling along the ancient streets of Jerusalem.

But again, I will let you go, dear tourist/occasional reader, wherever you want. Who am I to give you a lecture about the real Israel? You are free to believe that Israel is responsible for Western civilisation's shortcomings. I don't want to start a debate. I'll let you go visit Jerusalem and Masada and Nazareth and Bethlehem, real places but fascinating because they're mentioned in a book, maybe the first book you ever read. It's true that the first book one read carries always some magic! The Bible was not my first book.

I would rather look for Anda. To find the ground-floor apartment that she rented two years ago and has now problems keeping it, I have to take Rabbi Akiva Street and pass by the School of Dance, an old English building with a paved courtyard and old jacaranda trees planted in a circle like a hora, now in bloom, giving the air a magical violet lightness and fragility. Now, I am not flying anymore. I like to walk the streets.

The streets here are narrow, one lane with even narrower sidewalks. The houses are modest, dating from late 1800, the simple renovations done with blue or copper paint kept their original colonial past, modest but chic. The small backyards are full of flowers and modern pottery, this being the center of Tel Aviv pottery artists.

Before I get to Ben Yehuda, I have to turn right on Raban Gamliel Street where the sidewalk is overtaken by parked cars, all tiny models since Israel is tiny and overly populated. Before getting to her fence, opposite her house, the pavement has a hole not yet repaired, maybe as a reminder of a lost shell not intercepted by the Israeli dome during the last Hamas attack, a shell that elegantly flew from Gaza to Tel Aviv as a birthday wish for long life for Anda's twenty-third birthday. The fence facing the pavement hole is overflowing with rich bougainvillea, the color of blood, and the house in the back is exposing a colorful graffiti showing an Israeli beauty, olive skinned, dark big eyes as in Disney movies, a Semitic elegant nose, and curly long hair. Her house's number is no. 4, a yellowish house with a closed balcony and a mosaic of white and grey sea pebbles on the wall facing the street. Two green garbage bins are left in the street, maybe for lack of space in the tiny garden. The garbage smells, putrefied by the intense heat of July, and the myriad of electric wires, like shredded umbrellas, are disturbing the bohemian air of the street.

I am in Anda's garden, the orange tree scent fighting with the garbage bins' pestilent odors. The blue of the sky is so low that the tree branches are piercing it in luminous holes of light. I feel like an intruder, ashamed like watching a peep show. Anda is still sleeping, and her sadness is floating like a halo in her small room.

She was born on Canada Day. She was a beautiful baby. She is beautiful now, a younger Rachel Weiss with a soul as a dead sea in a Dali dream. She is not alone. As usual in between boyfriends, she is sharing her bed with an adopted pet. She still regrets losing Grace, the old bulldog she saved three years ago. In bed even if it's noon, Anda is now petting her last street acquisition, a black dog named Diva, while contemplating quitting her job. She is working night shifts at a hostel not far from here to be able to pay the rent because her parents, in fact her mom, decided to cut the umbilical cord. She is not surprised. She is the big sister, the black sheep of the family, and not yet graduated as expected.

Anda closes her blue eyes, misty from an imaginary cry. She feels, like every now and then, that she is born to the wrong parents in the wrong country. She was dreaming something about her mom, something new and unexpected as a hug or a smile. In real life, her mom is always wearing a sneer, and Anda is not able to face it anymore. She is stretching, eyes blinded by the sun, bathing in the dark scent of the orange tree, but the past is washing her face like an icy rain:

"You are too fat. You are ugly. You are dumb!" her mom used to scream at her when she was only three years old.

"Anda, you are a whale already! Stop eating like a cow! Look at you!" her mom used to scream at her when she was thirteen.

"You are a shame. You have to do your army service. Only the crazy or the Orthodox Jews are exempted. You are normal. You are dreaming that you have PTSD!" her mom screamed at her when she was eighteen.

"All you need from us is money, money, money. I will treat you as a teenager if I want to. Do you have an income? No. Are you self-sufficient? No. Are you forgetful and unconsiderate? Yes. This is the definition of a teenager!" Her mom is still screaming at her now.

Her mom never shed a tear, at least Anda doesn't remember it. Her mom never said "I love you" to her. Every time Anda sees a movie, reads a book, or just sees a mother and a daughter on the street hugging and saying, "I love you," her eyes get misty. She never had that. The "I loveyou" whispered under pressure once by her mom in the shrink's office where Anda spent two years in Tipul doesn't count in Anda's eyes.

I should be neutral like a real narrator, but I am an impostor, and I feel the urge to stroke Anda's hair, to hug her, to look into her eyes made of sky-liquid air, and tell her with momentary conviction, "Sweetie, everything will be fine!" Today, I lost my conviction after years of selling her from afar the prescriptions for happiness: "Forget the past. Stop trying to control everything. Don't blame anybody," all amazing ideas that Coelho, Wayne Dyer, the Dalai Lama, Linda Hay, and Miquel Ruiz put together.

Anda is not able to sleep anymore. It is too hot, and Diva is asking for her food. Diva is a funny name for a wonder dog, but Anda also is a strange name for a Jewish girl born in Israel. She hates her own name, almost a stigma. How in the name of the Lord did her mom, who decides everything in their house, choose Anda, not Shulamit, not Tova, not Sigalit as if to condemn Anda for a sin? This name is like a statement of rebellion, her mom's rebellion. Her mom's name is Monica, also a statement of secular Jewishness. Her mom could have changed her name to a Jewish name when she arrived in Israel from Romania, but she didn't consider it as many other Romanian Jews did. Her mom believed that in Israel you don't have to assimilate because you are not supposed to be discriminated like in the Diaspora.

Before going to the bathroom, she stretches again her body, now slim from a regimen of diet and yoga. Thank God for yoga and the people she met in Tel Aviv since she left Haifa. When she was eighteen, she knew she didn't want to do army service, and she didn't want to study in Haifa and stay home. Anda invokes in vain her memories of the shelling, the masks, and the tiny tent of her sister during the Gulf War in the '90s when she was only two. Her mother was convinced that Anda couldn't remember the two days of siege before fleeing the war and going to Montreal. Anda knows her memories are clear and her nightmares vivid. When she used to wake up during the night, she would hear a muffled sound of crying coming from her parents' bedroom or from their neighbor's, a single mom and a Lebanon war widow from Poland. At eighteen, Anda had to flee to Canada to her aunt (me) in an attempt to stay there and study after failing to convince her parents that she was afraid of the military service. She couldn't stay and study in Canada, but she returned to Israel a pariah, with a psychology recommendation in hand that she was sick with post-traumatic stress disorder, a diagnosis easier to obtain in Montreal, a city not yet recovered from Lepine's Poly 1986 attack.

When she moved to Tel Aviv University to study psychology and social science, she felt like a convict finally having her parole, but her freedom didn't help her get better. Freedom was not enough; she had and lost three boyfriends in two years, all tired of her obsessive and suffocating demands as they put it.

Anda found solace in yoga and supporting groups, usually composed of females and gays. She is now an avid user of safe spaces on the campus. The man she is looking for is outside somewhere, a strong and confident man, nothing like her father. But her first choices are always the animals, stray dogs and cats. She saves them, cleans them, feeds them, and loves them. And out of money, she places them in a shop for sell. Almost every term, she has a new pet friend. They never complain when she forgets to feed them or to leave them enough water. They are happy when they go for a stroll; they look into her eyes like she is the most beautiful human being. When they are curling around her in bed, a heavy fog is lifted from her chest, and the air becomes lighter, the orange flower scent clean as a cold mountain water. Her muscles are relaxing, and she can fall asleep without any drug. Today, on her birthday, she feels tired of the present and obsolete for the future. She needs five hundred shekels to be able to pay her rent for July, but she has no idea how to get them.

A stale coffee is waiting for her on the table from last night. Before going to work, she drinks it like a shooter. She chooses a blue tank top and a pair if white shorts from the pile of cleaned laundry on the floor, in the space between the coffee table and the flat TV. Her place is homey; she fits perfectly here, an old swing chair, a sofa-bed covered by a Romanian quilt, a small desk in one corner, a pot with a sabra cactus in the other corner. There is no door between her kitchen and the multipurpose room. Only a big Canadian flag separates the room and the kitchenette. She always believed that because she was born on Canada Day, she has to leave Israel and live in Canada, the land of peace and clean air.

Anda has conflict in her veins and in her genes, and she is still hoping to find a no-conflict zone in the outside world. She always had a seventh or eighth sense, the sense of the future, like a visionary

Greek oracle that saw the darkness when she took the pulse of the earth in trepidation. To leave Israel for Canada now is too late. The Israeli conflict is everywhere. Those young brainwashed Muslims and their suicide bombs are invincible while she and her friends from the support groups are overqualified with at least two diplomas but fragile and bendable as reed is in a strong wind. She and her yoga friends are hungry for love, an impotent love against the hate around them.

Two weeks ago, at her Friday yoga class, she met a boy. He was dark skinned, fit, and quiet. He was a regular for one month or so. Not many men were regulars. One day, he chose to put his mat close to hers. At the end of the class, he gently touched her right shoulder to tell her something. She looked for a second into his eyes, and she felt like a warm wave was flowing under her skin.

"You lost your hairband. I like your hair," he said, his voice low and soft as black velvet, his eyes fixing her so hard, it almost got her dizzy.

"Thanks. What's your name? A man at yoga, it's rather rare," she said.

"Nasser. Hmmm. I prefer yoga to going to the mosque," he said shyly, almost ashamed.

A long silence followed. Anda was not realizing that she was lost looking at his dark face, his dark eyes, trying to understand. To cut the awkward moment, Nasser continued, "What's your name? You look familiar to me."

"Ahh yes, I don't know. I don't believe we ever met. My name is Anda," she said, for the first time not ashamed about her name. They chatted for a while to discover they were both born in Haifa and they went to high school together. She couldn't stop thinking she was too fat back then even for him to notice her. She found out he was an Israeli Palestinian Muslim born in Ayra, the low part of the city, not on Neve Shannan Hill like her. Ayra had been poor and dirty before. Now it became clean and full of fancy restaurants. They separated waving.

Anda liked him from the first time she saw him one month ago. She liked his quietness and his concentration to get the right postures. Now, talking to him, she felt free, not pressured or scared. The fact that he was a Muslim was liberating in a strange way. They could never end up together; he cannot hurt her. They can be friends.

Anda is looking at her face imprisoned in the mirror and starts dancing on an imaginary Michael Jackson's song, "Black or White." She likes now what she sees, more than before, but she is not Rachel Weiss definitely. Anda suspected that her aunt (me) is using all kind of tricks to infuse some life into her dry soul. Anda knows she is nobody. She felt like a nobody since her mom complained to friends, neighbors, coworkers about Anda's weight even when Anda was present. Weight is a weight on Anda's shoulders and soul forever, but she finally gotten where her mom wanted her to be, as slim as her younger sister, Hanna.

Hanna is perfect, and Anda knows that she paved the way for this angel. Hanna doesn't like confrontation. She listens. She chose Technion instead of Tel Aviv University. She lives home and likes it. She has the same boyfriend since she was sixteen. She was a teen tennis Israel champion, and she did two years of military service without blinking. Even when Hanna got scared of Technion after failing her first term and decided to take a break of two years, her mom didn't scream at her.

Anda's gut is coming up from her throat like vomit when she thinks about it, but now she learns to face her fears even if she is afraid of war, afraid of bombs, afraid of love, afraid of religion, afraid of the future, afraid to be stabbed in her sleep one night like the little girl from Kiryat Arba in the occupied territories. One night a crazy Nasser might come in through her open window and slit her throat.

"How come nobody sees what Islam does to people? Why are other poor, oppressed, bombarded, or killed people, i.e., Vietnamese, Africans, Haitians, not violent? They might hate the West and Israel in the first place, but they don't kill. It's a shame that everybody talks freely about the Jewish conspiracy, the known slogan "Hollywood, the press, and finances are controlled by Jews" but only a few are ready to accept the danger of Islamic propaganda and education. The mosques are not places of cults, but schools of hate," Anda talks with Diva who is wagging her tale while eating.

Anda hoped that the Palestinian people from the Diaspora would be progressive, secular, educated, and determined to have a real country like the Jewish people had been for the last hundred years.

Even if, at Tel Aviv University 30 percent of students are Palestinians or Druze, she didn't make friends with any Muslim. She tried, but they kept away from her. Anyhow, most of them looked angry. Nasser didn't look angry.

She explained to Diva, "The Palestinians started throwing rocks when I was born, followed with suicide bombs in malls and buses during my teens, and now they take pleasure, together with ISIS-indoctrinated Muslims, slitting thirteen-year-olds' throats in their sleep. Why doesn't the world see it? Why does the world consider Israel a conspiracy but is blind to Muslims dancing in ecstasy after an ISIS terrorist attack? Somebody said that a nation's progress is judged by how they treat their pets. By the way, I love you, Diva, but ISIS men might not like you at all. In fact, every nation should be judged by how it treats their Jews."

Anda, a wonderful creation of arteries, veins, flesh, neurons, and dreams, once, twenty-five years ago, was only an egg lost in her mom's womb, a womb undecided when to ovulate over a three-month period of crazy hormones and no menstruation. This egg changed Monica from within. Anda was the most beautiful baby ever, a round body, a round face, the same big jaws as her father, a big smile under blue eyes inherited from Monica's father. As a toddler, Anda was a curious and feisty little girl with attitude. She was chunky and bold. Why, nobody knows, but Monica started turning an unexplained anger against her newborn, hurting her constantly and never short of insults.

Anda has read many books on borderline personality, and by now, she knows her mom fits the profile. The only question is how to protect yourself from your mom? Sometimes, Anda feels compassion for the Palestinian suicide bombers. They also have borderline moms like hers, showing only tough love in the name of Allah.

Her parents will be back tomorrow from their annual trip to Europe, and her father will try again to get the family together for her twenty-fifth birthday. She is sick of it. She cannot take it anymore. After every family gathering, she feels as if she is beaten with a bag of rice, her skin is cold as a lizard, and she cannot sleep for two nights. She has to make peace with herself alone, completely alone from now on, alone in an effervescent city, alone in a crazy Israel, alone in a murdering world.

She has to understand why her mom is the way she is, but who to ask? The few who know are dead or far away. Her mom's mom died of cancer when Anda was only two years old. She doesn't remember her grandma. Her mom never told them stories about her grandma. She bottled everything inside. Anda had to guess, and just from looking at her grandma's pictures, she knows she was beautiful and tough, carrying on her shoulders the pain of so many generations of Sephardi Jews migrating from place to place, from Spain to Turkey, from Turkey to Romania, and finally to Israel. Anda knows only that her grandma was tired of migrating. She loved Romania and didn't want to leave for Israel.

I have to forgive my mom. She loves me, but maybe she is afraid to tell me. The good voice in Anda's head whispered, *I am the baby that came at the same time as my grandma's cancer. Maybe my mom felt betrayed by life and by having me had to give up her own mom, an impossible bargain, a new life and a future death.*

Jewish stories are always sad because of the bloody Nazis! Anda thinks. She remembers now the silent cry in the night that used to be part of her nightmares, a cry coming from her parents' bedroom, like the cry of a pilgrim mourning when he finally arrives to his destination.

Anda feels her body alive and strong, a body suddenly light like a feather. She rips off the Canadian flag as if unveiling an imaginary idol, and she goes straight to the garbage can in front of her house. While letting the cheap plastic cloth, white like a shirt spotted with a huge stain of blood, fall inside and scare the stray cats, making them jump as if a bomb raid just started, she admires the red explosion of the bougainvillea across the street. She has to survive as did her ancestors in even worst conditions. Israel is her home. She will find her mom's love no matter how deep she has to dig and how long she has to wait.

4

A GOOD DEED

Paris

I am sitting in the Delta waiting area in Charles de Gaulle Airport to board my plane back home. I still have five hours to kill, and I feel as if Paris was a bribe for a God I don't believe in. I am watching people passing by, some walking, others running, all having a strange look like lost bees in a room full of smoke. The air is saturated with croissant smell and the fragrance of French perfumes. Slim and elegant women are passing by with idle confidence. Three backpackers are sitting across from me on the floor, drinking espresso in tiny cups. Coffee shops, salads, sandwiches, croissants, drinks, newspapers, books, all overpriced; exhausted commuters lying down on uncomfortable chairs with handles, impossible to get to a bearable position to sleep. I bet everybody is secretly praying to get home in one piece.

My eyes are burning, and my head is spinning from the lack of sleep and the airport's disturbing murmur as if a sea flooded the floor beneath us. I am trying to close my eyes, but I feel like an owl sitting on a branch, dreaming with my eyes wide open.

I just left Delia at her gate. She is going back to Bucharest. Before we split, I explained for a second time the meaning of every letter and number on her boarding pass. I assured her that I will send the pictures in no time. I took her in my arms, and I whispered in her ear, "We had a good time. You will see everything will turn out all right. Life is full of surprises, not only bad ones." Delia didn't buy it, and I saw her eyes getting misty. I turned my back saying, "As soon as I get home, I will call you to know you got home all right!" I knew I wouldn't do it. I was exhausted but relieved.

I just heard her whispering, "I will pray for you!" without knowing why. Maybe she wanted to be grateful and this was her only power.

"I need a lot of prayers" came out of my mouth, more like a sigh.

I have no religion, I lost it long time ago, and I never found it again, it was easier this way to accept my misdemeanors. I speak four languages, but none well enough. I am a product of multiple immigrations and a lost soul in a cold country, forever carrying a backpack of dried-up nostalgia, a mother tongue that doesn't feel mine anymore and some nice pictures from the Romanian countryside. Delia, on the other hand, knows only one language. She goes to church every Sunday, and she is active in Romanian politics, politics that I completely ignore, being too murky for my taste.

We are now both as old as our grandma was when we first met. Back then, we were little girls, and now, look at us, fifty years later, our souls trapped in some uninspired Halloween costumes. We have the same genes, the same laugh, the same walk, the same wrinkles, the same taste in almost everything, and we complete without effort each other's sentences. Delia is tough and harsh, and compared to her, as my husband says, I am too good, almost dumb. She is the clever one. I am the lucky one! She is in Romania trying to make ends meet. I am living in Palo Alto and I am well fed. She has been divorced for twenty years. I have been married for thirty-five years. She has an unstable son suffering from a major depression. I have two responsible boys who both have jobs. She has a small decrepit apartment in Bucharest that feels like a prison to her because she has to split it with her son until she dies. I have two houses, two cars, and a good job in the USA.

I travel a lot for my job, and it just happened I had a three-day meeting in Paris. I offered her to come and stay with me for a week for old time's sake. I got this idea to meet in Paris, between Palo Alto and Bucharest, at the last minute. I tried to bring her to California two years ago, but her tourist visa request was turned down. Anyhow, she was not ready yet to leave her son alone for a month or so. Also, us being together in our house in Palo Alto would have been annoying for my husband. Radu needs his silence, his sleep, and his space, and we are *noisy* when together. Radu was already neurotic before getting the cancer, now he needs my constant protection.

Paris was my gift to her, a gift to make up for a mistake that I made six months ago. Back then, I didn't believe it was a mistake to play God. It turned out that my good deed was a mistake that didn't let me sleep last night, our last night together.

We spent our last evening on the tiny terrace of the studio we shared for one week in Paris. We had a light French supper, green salad, some good cheese, foie gras, and cheap champagne. Cheap is fine with me. I like the taste of cheap because when I pay a lot, I have high expectations and I cannot enjoy it. Finally, after a grey week of May in Paris, the dusk was covering the city with a sky rosy as a baby's cheek. The terrace was overlooking an elegant cemetery that reminded us of our childhood, how scared we were passing by the village cemetery and laughing to overcome the fear. We were not scared anymore. We just enjoyed the view and us being together. We inhaled the sunset's perfume. The air was heavy with bright colors and smelled like Bucharest's streets after rain, and we were unable to explain why. Paris was Delia's first trip abroad. She is fearless, but travelling alone from Bucharest to Paris was a big step for her. "Oh, boy, Delia! You did it, girl ! To fly Bucharest-Frankfurt-Paris for the first time in your life without knowing any English or French is a challenge sometimes," I said proud of my Delia, my mirror image.

"Flying was a piece of cake. Waiting for you and being afraid to exit was the scary part!" she giggled.

Indeed. One week ago, we had both been scared to death while being separated by the sliding frosted glass of the exit doors of Terminal D at De Gaulle Airport. I was responsible for the disaster! I had made our travel plans, making sure I will arrive in Paris first to pick up Delia up at her gate and I will depart after her to be able to let her at her gate, but I overlooked the fact that we were arriving at different terminals. Delia had no information except that she had to wait for me inside the terminal. We had been unable to communicate, our cells from different continents and providers. To call my husband and wake him up was out of question. Praying was more appropriate. Nothing worked—free airport Wi-Fi to send e-mails to her son in Romania, airport announcements on loud speakers, or screaming her name through the exit doors while giving the impression I was crazy. Who saved us? A dark-skinned immigrant on a Segway going in and out of the sliding doors of the luggage claim area through her terminal.

I asked him to go back inside and look for "me" on the other side, a "me" with orange hair and bigger butt. When I saw her coming out followed closely by our savior, I started jumping like a kid. We didn't know how to thank Ibrahim, our savior! Our laugh was more of a nervous laugh, with tears of relief as if we had flown for an hour through turbulences and almost died. But who cares for two old fools like us?

"What a good story to share over champagne on a Parisian terrace overlooking a cemetery!" I said. We started laughing, remembering our childhood fears when we were sent to sleep in the guest room at her parents' home and we couldn't sleep terrified by the trees shadows bent by the fall winds. I still remember putting my head under the pillow so that I would not see the outside monsters anymore and the joy of inhaling the bedsheets' lavender and mint scent before entering sleep. My aunt's skirt, Delia's mom, had the same smell.

I was happy with our studio rental I had found with homelidays. com near Da Vinci University walking distance from La Defense. The studio, slick and modern, more or less a box in North American standards, made us feel young again. We had everything we needed on a twenty-square-meter surface. It felt cozy and equally hilarious with an elevated kitchen and a bar table literally above the bed, a bed we found full of crumbles at night when we dropped dead from too much walking and talking.

During the first three days while I was in meetings, Delia took the metro and visited Paris on her own, the majestic Paris, tour Eiffel, Le Louvre, Champs- Élysées. The last three days, we spent together at my favored places, the Paris for artists and writers, Montmartre, Quartier Latin, Café de Flore, Jardin Luxembourg, Le Marais, Place des Vosges and la Chapelle. We took a bus and a *bateau mouche* tour.

We didn't want to talk about our sons on purpose. We wanted to fully enjoy Paris and be together. We wanted to feel young and careless. Our legs were hurting, but we kept laughing. We made the same sounds of pain and relief when sitting down in the metro after a long day of wandering through the labyrinth of Paris's elegant order. The evenings were cold, the air clean but we felt relaxed as if we were taking a bubble bath together. During the day, Paris in May had a subtle and mysterious smell.

Paris was my gift to her. In fact, I had helped her financially for the last twenty years or so, but this time I decided to give her something for her soul, something less material. If I sent her money, I knew she would keep it in a secret place, waiting for the unexpected problems her future holds. I cannot blame her. She had it rough, and what could be rougher than being a single mom to a sick boy who doesn't want to grow up? I have to say that my husband had never been cynical about Delia, and he approved of me helping her.

Since the day we met and till I left Romania thirty years ago, Delia and I, spent almost every summer together. In many ways, Delia knew me more than anybody else. She had to. She had been there for me at every turn of my life. I had done the same. Maybe our destiny was written during those summers together. Back then, I remember thinking that my family was not as much fun as hers. I was the only kid, and my parents were very strict on studying. Delia was the only daughter of Didina, my aunt from my father side, a skinny woman with a big frown and rarely a smile, a woman I never understood how she was able to work the field from 5:00 AM to 5:00 PM. Delia had less pressure to study. She had three older brothers, and she was supposed to help around the house, but in her case, the chores were not a joke. She had to feed the animals, a cow, three goats, a dozen of chickens, and a dog. She had to clean. She had to wash. She had to milk the cow. She had to bike to bring the cheese from sheep farm, to pick up the corn from the fields or the raisins from the vineyard. Sometimes I felt she was kind of a slave, a slave who had more freedom than I had, always on a bike. I didn't have a dog or a bike. I was only a poor city girl. In fact, I didn't even know how to ride a bike. When she finally taught me, I was fourteen and had been in love for so many times by now. At that time, she still hated boys.

Right from the beginning, we let the other enter our souls, and have never let go. When I first met her, she was five years old, and she was hiding in our great-grandma's room, in the corner behind the door.

"Adriana, go to see great-Grandma. She has a surprise for you," my grandma told me.

I didn't like going into the elderly woman's room. I was afraid of her. She was 102, in my eyes almost dead, dressed in black, and always sleepy. The whole family was proud that she was so old, and they used to say that she was just pretending to be asleep or senile, but that she knew everything that was happening around her. She was the perfect witness.

I didn't like the old lady who never spoke. I entered the room anyway, my heart shrinking. I looked around, still feeling the coldness of the door handle shaped like a metal leaf. I saw a pile of covers on the bed, no soul around, and I ran to my grandma saying, "Your mom is sleeping. I didn't see anything in there."

"Adriana, try again," she said. "Delia, don't be afraid! Get out of there!" she screamed to an imaginary ghost.

I went again to confront the ghost, and a copy of myself appeared from behind the door. I liked her instantly. She was five, shy, blond, tanned, no freckles.

"Adriana does not bite, you wild village girl. Delia, Adriana is your cousin from Bucharest," said our grandma. "Go play, go, go!" she added.

We both adored our grandma. She never spoked much—our grandpa was the talker—but everything she said stayed with us for life. She was a force. Compared to her, we are still driving through life with a sign on the bumper: "I am a beginner."

Delia told me how she felt when we first met. She was speechless because somebody like me, from Bucharest, was like a foreigner to her. She was intimidated and curious. I remember that Delia impressed me from the first moment. Before going to play with her in the cornfield, pretending to be mom and dad, I had to go to the toilet. At our grandma's, the toilet was outdoor in the middle of the enclosed hen quarters. Grandma had five or six turkeys that I was afraid of. They used to surround me making scary noises. I preferred peeing in the cornfield. When I told Delia, she started laughing and somehow, her laugh encouraged me.

I still remember the magic that we saw in us, time expanding when we were together, exploring and opening our hearts like do poppies in wheat field in May. We were putting our feelings in the palm of our hands to show to the other a time when the air was thin and easy to breathe, the rain rich, the moon as big and bright as an illuminated pumpkin. I still remember the sweetness of our breakfast, milk with noodles, left by my aunt in the blinding sunny morning of July in a clay pot on the wooden table underneath the walnut tree in front of their house. This was a time the rainbow was constantly in our eyes as when we were lying down in the cornfield, filling our lungs with the scent of seeds, buds, wild flowers, and fruits, of the air at noon or the humid air after rain while playing the rainbow game invented by me; we had to close our eyes facing the sun and try to see a certain color just by playing with the muscles of our eyelids. A shut eye meant black; an almost open lid meant bright yellow, and so on. Somewhere in between, we were fighting to find the purple red.

At the second bottle of cheap champagne, with our dilated pupils reflecting a last image of Paris together, we started to talk about the men we loved or hated. We never kept secrets from each other. She knew when I was in love the first time at thirteen. His name was Sorin. He loved the Beatles and drawing. She knew when my first love left Bucharest to relocate with his parents to another city in Romania whose name I don't remember. She knew about my first kiss at a party when I was fifteen and how I hated it. He was older and salivating when he forced his tongue into my throat. She knew about my first sex encounter at eighteen, the fight and the loss. She knew I loved my husband to death but he had disappointed me and ripped me off having a happy family. She knew I loved another man, and that man had implored me to leave my husband, something I decided not to do because no mother in her right mind would sacrifice her kids like that. I knew when she was in love for the first time at sixteen. I knew every moment of her passionate relationship with her first husband, an alcoholic writer that she had the willpower to leave. I knew how desperate she had been to have a family and her joy when she had a boy two years after I had my second. Hers would become the love of her life. I knew how life turned her good decisions into mistakes and my mistakes into good decisions. Life had changed us, but not our friendship.

I even tried helping her to immigrate to California fifteen years ago after her divorce from her second husband and her son's father.

Out of spite, her ex didn't agree to let their son leave, and she had to stay in Romania. Since then, I helped her with money, clothes, and meds. Till recently, she was the same size as me, and it was pleasant to know there was an image of me walking the Bucharest streets.

I would have like to tell her about Tudor, but I was ashamed and afraid that I would spoil the spell he put on me. Besides, I needed more time to really understand why I feel what I feel for Tudor. I needed more time to know Tudor. I felt guilty that I sent Tudor to her like a prize. I felt guilty I presented her to Tudor as an easy prey for fooling around. It was not my intention. I wanted to put a ray of light into their lives.

The sun was almost gone. We were searching for the moon to find moral support, but we couldn't see it yet, the buildings around us too tall. We had the feeling that we got wise too late. We loved, and we didn't know how to appreciate our men. We were too feisty and too demanding. She knew that I fell out of love with my husband a long time ago because I didn't know better. In time, I realized that he is a good man even if he is neurotic. Maybe I was afraid that a divorce would be too messy. Maybe I believed that real happiness was overrated, or maybe I preferred to channel my energy differently. I told her that now I forgive him, but it is too late to rebuilt. We are just patching. I love him now kind of halfway, like two people who once knew each other well but now are separated by a busy highway. We don't share every moment of our lives. We just have a long-term project together. He is not able to travel, to do sports, or even to take a walk with our dog, too tired and angry all the time. It's strange that his illness, a cancer under control, didn't make him hungry to live, but hungry to be still. I respect his wishes by leaving him alone in his safe space at home. We understand, finally, that we are different, and none of us will change.

Delia is not a woman of half measures; she loved and left her first and true love. She admitted that she didn't have enough patience with men. She left two husbands, the first one because she loved him too much, the second one because she didn't love him enough. Ironically, now she has no choice. With her sick son, she is his prisoner. Delia was always jumpy and quick to judge people, and I liked that. It was something I never mastered. I am a pro in if's and maybe's. I am also the only one to know that she was only seventeen when she took care of her dying mother. I am the only one to know that she was raped not long after her mother died and when this happened, she didn't even suffer much, maybe because she was dead inside, maybe because she didn't care about her body. Maybe it was only a test to see if she was still alive.

We raised our glasses to our grandma who used to say, "Everybody has to carry his cross." What a stupid saying! We used to laugh when we were young! Now, we understand. Delia has a huge cross to carry while I feel more like a puppet controlled by a puppeteer's cross.

"You know, I went to bed with Tudor six months ago," Delia said, and it felt like lightning just touched my skin branching out on my face and chest like weed. I was completely silent, and for a moment, I felt as we were playing "statues," a game of our youth—I touch you; you don't move. Something shoots through my brain at the speed of light, and I barely moved my lips thinking, *What the hell do I do now?* I felt a moment of grace as if I was walking a fine line over the abyss. I decided to let her talk to gain time and to regroup. This was the first time in my life I kept something from her, and the reason was Tudor. Tudor was my treasure.

"Really? I was kind of hoping you would hit it off. Good for you! Delia, you can only be a mother for so long. You deserve to be a woman again," I said, my words sounding like thunder. I felt dizzy as if hit by a strong wind. To keep my balance, I took a sip from my glass of champagne, a champagne that now tasted like sand.

"I was ashamed to tell you, and I asked him not to tell you," she said.

"You guys succeeded to keep the secret. He told me nothing. How was it with him? Did you like it?" I asked, telling myself how good I am at hiding it, my heart pounding.

"I didn't like it. I felt he wanted only to score. He disgusted me. I didn't feel anything. We went to a hotel after we had supper in a restaurant in Cismigiu. He bought a bottle of cheap wine on our way to the hotel. He was cheap in general. He told me his wife doesn't sleep with him anymore. I didn't really care. His confession felt out of place, like begging. He even took Viagra before getting into bed with me." She put all her cards on the table. I trusted her.

"Good at least you tried," I encourage her with a low voice as if talking to my chin.

"I know now that sex is not for me. Tudor was my validation," she said, closing an open door with a bang. I almost wanted to say that she needed time to know a man and a life time to know herself, but it was too much of a lecture. Her Tudor was not my Tudor.

Not long ago, Tudor was my best friend at work. It helped that we were both from Romania. We knew each other for almost ten years. We played volleyball together, and we were taking walks at noon during lunch. We chatted about everything, family, kids, society, work, weather, health—you name it. When he first confessed about his wife, I was not surprised; after all, everybody knew me as Mother Teresa and confessed to me sooner or later. It's true that this was intimate, but we were good friends and I was not prudish. We knew by now that our marriages weren't perfect, but whose was? We both believed in marriage no matter what. We were on the same page. Changing life partners is too easy of a fix, a fix chosen by immature people.

I decided to help Tudor. This is me, as my grandma put it, "Adriana, you are like honey for the weak and crazy." Helping people is my obsession, but maybe it is a penchant of all immigrants. When you are an immigrant, you get to your adoptive country completely unprepared as if you are born a second time. You have no roots, you don't get any of the jokes, and you don't know how to swear, and on top of it, you are short on time. You have to compensate for not being born there, accumulate money, houses, cars, and positions at a double speed. Some immigrants are disappointed. Some are struggling. Some are using the system. Some hate the system. Some return. Some adapt, but almost all of them are damaged by the move, all the family's ties severed, grandkids without grandparents, parents dying alone, or even worse, living alone.

When I arrived in the USA, I discovered my passion, maybe because I felt lucky and I needed to give back or to give away a love of no use. A complete stranger, a friend of a friend of a friend, a chain of Romanians, Jews and Romanian Jews helped us when we arrived in Palo Alto in the spring of '90 and showed me how to do it. Since then, I had helped any Romanian or any Jew immigrant that knew somebody who knew me. Lately, because I ran out of immigrants to help, I have a new profile. I am hooking up singles whose lives are too busy or who had just given up on looking for somebody.

One year ago, Tudor became more unsettled about the problem in his marriage, his perfect wife refusing him any intimacy by then; they got to a point that they only did it twice a year on vacation. He walked and talked like a broken man. His parents were in Romania, and every fall he used to visit them alone. He knew Delia because every year, I had asking him to bring her money from me. I liked Tudor, and Delia liked him too back then. For me, Tudor had substance and a comforting presence. He never struck me as macho, more like a funny and easygoing guy like any other Romanian man. Somehow, he was intriguing to me. He had a subtle sweetness I couldn't explain, but I didn't have time to ponder on it. Delia had a different perception; to her, he was a real player, trying to poke women to get their attention.

In my simple or twisted mind, one and one makes two; I had two good friends in my life, two people I cared for, both unhappy in their way, a man and a woman in search of some tenderness. Eureka! Let's get them together! Delia was without a man for twenty years and absorbed by her son's universe of depression and medication while Tudor lost any closeness to the love of his life, his wife. He made me understand that making love was not only painful for his wife, but she was also kind of scared of any sign of tenderness, a prelude to sex, a torture to her. I didn't believe it in the beginning, but as a woman, I kind of understood that drifting away is possible. Being sixty, not having intimacy for such a long time, getting closer to the finish line, and being in need for some timid signs of love, even a surrogate love, all these can make you bend the moral narrative a little, I thought.

I let Tudor understand that he could try to go to bed with Delia. Why not? His marriage wouldn't be in jeopardy, on the contrary. I wanted to save his marriage. After all, he was a man, and I saw so many men his age leaving their wives for some fresh meat, some as young as thirty years old. I didn't want this to happen to him, being pushed against the wall. Delia liked him—I knew it. He liked Delia—he had told me. He also told me that we looked and sounded the same. He was like a prisoner in his house in the USA. Delia was a prisoner in Romania, in her country, city, and apartment. Both deserved a human touch. I understood that he wasn't looking for a one-night stand or a prostitute, but for closeness and acceptance. He went to Romania and came back telling me he didn't sleep with Delia.

I looked at my soul sister's face. Delia's eyes were full of disappointment. I wished she had felt good with Tudor, a Tudor that was not mine yet six months ago. I showed her the two empty bottles, and told her we have to go to bed. We lay down side by side, now even more tied together this time by the same man. I faked sleeping, imagining our grandma looking at us from behind the moon and laughing at how stupid we turned in our old age.

I played God with two human beings that I cared for, and God played me back good. I felt like a sex offender, a liar, a prostitute, and a pimp all combined for a good deed.

How strange! Delia hated Tudor now, but I was falling in love with him.

Questions without answers didn't let me sleep: Why didn't he tell at the time? We were just friends six months ago. How come Delia and I, we have such different feelings for the same man? He loves me? Or is he playing around with old desperate women? Am I a joke for him? Who is whos surrogate, am I hers, or she is mine? Am I stupid? Am I too soft? Am I dumb? Is Delia one of many women he slept with or was she only a way to have me, a love he couldn't get? Did I sell out Delia? Did I sell out a part of me? When he was in bed with Delia, was he dreaming about me? Why did I fall in love with him after his trip to Romania?

All I had felt last November was a jolt to be reborn after a long dead winter. It was more powerful than me. I was longing for him like a drug addict. My core was somewhere between my heart and my thighs.

I am becoming one of those promiscuous ladies from old people residences, without any barriers, no principles, only carnal desire, the final desire before you go. Why do I feel protected in his arms? Why do I feel understood? Why do I feel complete when making love to him?

All this was unbearable. The bedsheets were burning my skin, my heart was pounding, my head was spinning, and his image begging for my tenderness was invading my scalp like a crown of black butterflies.

What should I do? Tudor played us both? Who played who? What should I believe? Believe him because he loves me and that makes him true or believe him because, even if he lies, his lies are beautiful?

But I saw the sorrow in his eyes. I had seen his delirium in lovemaking. I saw his body like a blade ready to snap, waiting for my reactions, afraid that I would say no.

As mothers, we are sweet and understanding with our sons' shortcomings. As women, we are cold and critical of any man proposing closeness to us, considering him a pig. In the end, every man needs a woman's touch and tenderness. Sex, as dirty as it might seem, is a search to get close, a hunger to be vulnerable, a desire to touch somebody's core, soul and skin. I was guided by my flesh and my gut to Tudor's soul. I found a diamond there.

I kept my secret because I didn't want to destroy my bond with Delia. I wanted to keep my eyes shut and see a rainbow again, but all I could see was a rainbow of white lies.

I fell asleep late, but Delia woke me up every hour. Her cell was still on Romanian clock, one hour behind Paris clock. My cell was even worst, still on U.S. time. It was more confusing to calculate the Paris time from it: do I have to add or to subtract instead? But I preferred the confusion to the effort to reset the time on Paris time and again in Palo Alto after my arrival. She kept waking up confused and afraid that we would be late at the airport.

The Delta gate is open now, and boarding is starting. Suddenly, I feel tired of caring for Delia. I remembered Tudor's reaction about Delia when I asked him once again to give her money from me. He told me, "You are helping her too much. She is not handicapped." This was one year ago, and I had thought, *What the hell does he know about me, about her? This is not his business.*

My sick husband is my priority now, but I need Tudor, a man I have no right to love, but his touch, his words, his hands, his lips, his body glued against mine are gentle like a breeze. Nobody touches me like Tudor. My husband's touch was like a hurricane leaving me devastated and empty every time. With age and his sickness, our intimate moments are more like a ghost of another life.

I know now that I am going back to an oasis that Tudor created for me, in a cozy hotel room by the bay where we will drink cheap wine, where we will touch our souls with a silky tenderness, where the only smell will be the luminous fragrance of our lovemaking, where the only music will be the softness of our yes, and where we will be connected to the real world by a rainbow of lies.

Palo Alto

While looking out the window to check if his backyard magnolia is still in bloom in spite of the unusually cold morning, Tudor cannot explain why, after so many years, Adriana had fallen for him. He had tried everything to get close to her, following her everywhere, playing ping-pong and volleyball with her, opening his heart, sending her songs that made him dream about her and waking up unable to breathe from desire. He hadn't even realized his love for her till a colleague told him, "You have eyes only for Adriana." But she had always been distant and inviting somehow, going through life like a wise woman fascinated by couples' ups and downs. Suddenly, a spark started a fire that consumed her and pushed her into his arms when he least expected. For some time now, he wore an uncontrollable smile, looking like a kid who got the toy he asked Santa for many years ago. He was a wounded man before last November. Now he felt complete, waiting for her to get back from Paris.

Bucharest

Delia was crying while landing at Otopeni, Bucharest's airport, afraid to go back to her life. Usually, after a few days with Adriana, she used to feel good as if her mother just hugged her, a mother without a frown, only a smile. To separate from Adriana was as difficult as in her childhood, but this time, she doesn't feel recharged. She has to go back and face the tyranny of her sick son. She has to survive like an inmate in her own home. She has to ask herself, again and again, the same question: what do I have to do to keep him sane? She has to lie again about her son's condition to be able to go out and face the world.

The sun is down, its violet light cold and dirty. She sighs, trying not to get vertigo from the heavy scent of flowers, flowers falling down from the linden trees and covering Bucharest's streets like snow. She has to carry a cross and only Adriana knows how heavy it is.

5

SKYPE IN TONGUES

Mornings like today are killing Milly. Her pain, as a morning lover, is cutting her in two. She just took her pills, but she has to wait for the relief to kick in. It is end of January in Montreal and winter is here again for good. The light coming in from her small window, like the window of a cell, is eerie at 6:00 AM. The air in her room is musty and has the smell of her heavy sleep. Milly is sitting on the edge of the bed, trying to control her lower muscles not to pee herself. Stefan, her casual roommate who sleeps in well after 10:00AM after watching porno movies every night, might dismiss her again, "You are old and disgusting. You should wear diapers." She knows, but she is postponing.

The winter gale is hauling at her windows, but she can hear her upstairs neighbors, Omama and Ibrahim, not from Romania like her but from Montenegro, getting up. Omama, the wife, is slowly going to the toilet. She is heavier than Milly and obsessed with cleaning. Milly hopes Omama won't do her washing today; otherwise, the pipe in Milly's bathroom will leak again. Omama's family are refugees from the Kosovo war and their English is much worse than Milly's. They don't know a word of French. Sometimes Milly has the impression that she's living in a Kusturica movie on a Canadian location, trapped between the bridge on the east, the St. Marie Church in the west, the main boulevard on the south, and St. Lawrence River on the north. Here, everybody is on welfare, and helping each other is a must. Jean from no. 4 is their cigarette provider, making a trip once a month to a native reservation to buy cheap. Andrew from no. 8 is their clothing provider. He collects everything big houses from Ile Bizard throw away. Milly is the pain killer provider. That's why, many times, by the end of the month, she has none left.

Nobody in her building has signed any lease with Sirti, their landlord, also from Montenegro. Everybody wants a break, Sirti from repairing, painting, or maintaining the apartments, the tenants from paying the rent on time. Sirti didn't repair her leaking pipe in the bathroom, but he gives her a lift to the bank every month to withdraw her rent money. Their street, Des Fraises, is part of a land where money is in shortage, iPads are a dream, the senses are impaired, and the air is cutting your skin like barbed wire; a land close to the border between two worlds, the rich and the poor, the healthy and the crippled, the sane and the crazy.

Milly's pain is not going away even after taking two extra-strength Aleves. When this happens, she feels the urge to roar like a wounded animal. Memories from another life are woven with this back pain, a sign of her humiliation. It is the end of the month, and she just took the last two pills. She is idle, staring at the wall in front of her at a picture of herself when she was twenty, a picture taken by Alex on the Romanian seashore at Eforie; she was wearing a white dress, her skin dark and shiny, smelling like peaches, her body light. She was dancing on the beach at dawn, her long chestnut hair flowing around her while she was swirling.

Sometimes, in her dreams, Milly can see her previous life as an outsider. She is driving by the old house. It is summer. The golden forsythia bushes, the red geranium pots hanging from the gutters, the rhododendrons, irises, and lilies explode around the pine tree in the middle of the lawn, their colors moving lightly in the air as in amber fluid. She sees Alex, her husband, washing the Volvo, their kids running in front of the house playing tag or spraying themselves with water guns, and Buddy, their dog, running in circles trying to catch his tail while bumping into the kids. Alex laughs, but Milly's mom, who lived with them till her death, has her face in her hands, standing in front of the entrance door, her body aligned with the tall clematis bush climbing the entrance stairs handrail.

Why is my mom crying? Why I am not in the picture? Milly asks herself as if she is a spectator. When her imaginary car passes by, she can smell happiness and fresh basil from the back garden. She misses her garden, her real flowers, the texture of their petals on the tip of her fingers, the smell of the lilies in May and of fresh tomatoes and cucumbers after rain in August. All she has kept is this image of her crying on the stairs and her scarf, a traditional Transylvanian scarf that she used to wear only at funerals.

She never dreams about the basement episode. She doesn't want to think about it, but often this memory jumps on her like a wolf. Everything started like a regular quarrel. By the end of their life together, Milly and Alex used to do it every day. It was their dynamic as if nothing was left of their tender moments when they were young and she used to cry during lovemaking, a fountain of happiness released in her navel while he was kissing her every toe like a slave. He was her first and only man. They had known each other since they were five or six years old playing together on the same street in Bucharest. They got married being in love—at least she was. Alex was handsome then. He was also a smart and proud man. His dream was to have many kids and a good income to keep his wife at home. His dream fit her well because she liked being protected. She didn't have ambitions or talents. Besides, she had trouble in school with reading, with languages, and with math, never able to concentrate for long. She was more of a hippy artsy type with a passion for flowers.

They had wanted kids badly, but for seven long years, she was not able to conceive. She entered a fertilization program, and her body became more of a lab or a shooting range where her eggs were being bombarded with higher and higher doses of hormones. Maybe her craziness started when doctors injected her with hormones that deformed her body to the point of no recognition, from a slim beauty to a heavy lady. The kids finally came, one after another, perfectly healthy, rushing to get through a slightly open door. But as if life made you pay for every happy moment, Alex's love dried up. His affection was now distributed as in many communicating vessels, the children's vessels were full, Milly's was empty.

Their lovemaking got weird and dirty—he wanted it from the back. Then she decided she was better off sleeping with the dog in another room. Milly was kind of proud about refusing sex.

When Milly casually told Vera at a BBQ party that they hadn't had sex in ten years, Vera was shocked. How could Alex not be crazy yet?

"Don't worry—he is crazy enough." Milly laughed.

"Milly, are you out of your mind torturing him like that? A man needs sex like he needs water," Vera said, but Milly knew better.

They ended up never meeting at night and hated each other openly during the day. Their house was a war zone where doors were slammed at a musical pace, a show that the kids, now ten and fourteen, seemed to have adapted to.

One morning, after the kids left for school and before his three employees had arrived, he called her from the basement where his IT business was. He told her to sit down and be quiet for a moment.

"Milly, I will be leaving this house," he told her with a low voice she could barely make out.

"Where? Did you find a new place for your shitty business?" she asked in a high-pitched voice, ready for an offensive.

"Milly, I am serious. I am divorcing you. Look at me! I cannot continue anymore. I did everything to make it better. We just came back from a long trip to Europe, and we are back to square one. I don't know what to do anymore, and I am trying my best to keep a straight face for the kids," he said matter-of-factly.

"Don't patronize me! You treat me like a slave! You wanted me at home with the kids, but you always complain that I don't do anything for this family!" she started screaming like a madwoman.

"What about me, Milly? You're too much of a lady to open your legs from time to time for your hardworking husband. Because of me, you are driving a Volvo. Thanks to me, the kids are going to a private school. Thanks to me, you had your mother living with us. Thanks to me, you've had it easy. Don't get me started!" he raised his voice into a howl.

She saw Buddy at the top of the basement stairs looking at them, his head tilted to one side with a questioning expression.

Alex, not knowing what to do with the anger strangling him, his face red, his hands trembling while and his veiny arms were pointing to the ceiling but not for long because he, started throwing the computers on the floor, one by one. "It's enough, enough, enough! I've had it with you. Tomorrow I am leaving, and I'm taking the kids with me. You'll be getting the divorce papers soon. You better get a lawyer," he said, his voice suddenly calm and low.

To regain strength, he sat down on their old olive leather couch, dismissed from the living room but good enough for the basement office. She couldn't remember ever seeing him so resigned and relieved. She felt her cheeks hot red and her limbs frozen, her heart writhing inside her chest. She felt tired as if she was swimming against a current.

She winced and saw herself taking his hand and kissing it in an almost rote move. She heard herself drawling, "Buuuuut ouuuur maaaaarriage is a gooood maaaarriage, Alex, no?"
"Are you kidding me? No, our marriage is hell, and I want out of this hell," he said with no shadow of a doubt.
"Please, stay! We have to try to fix it," she begged, kissing his hand again and, not really knowing why, remembering what Vera told her about a man needing sex like water.

She looked at him as if seeing him for the first time in years, and she realized she hadn't paid attention to his grimaces and scowling demeanor. She was just protecting herself, looking away, trying to get away from him, touching him being out of question as if he was full of pus. Many times she felt the desire to put a pillow over his head during his sleep, a desire crossing her mind for a split second like a mental blink.

He stood in front of her with a look of disgust. While she looked into his eyes trying to understand him, he spat on her. She didn't care about the spit, she was hypnotized by the truth when their eyes met. Everything was there, the plain truth, their stupid quarrels that ate at them from the inside, a hunger for hate eating away whatever happy moments they had before the decline.

He left, and she winced at every slamming door, the basement door, the door of the bathroom, after a while the door of his bedroom, and finally the front door. Milly felt like a bug being squashed in the hinge of the front door. She was alone with Buddy in an empty house that had to be sold. She stood there like she was forever in a cave, slightly above ground, her world washed away. No tears had been shed. She felt out of place and entitled to act like a crazy person. This time, Buddy was the one who stopped her from going to the bathroom and counting her painkillers. Buddy came down the stairs and put his head on her lap. She remembered what her kids, her kiiiiddddssss, were saying only a few days ago: "Mom, you and Daddy should separate. We don't want to see you mad at each other all the time!" Only the dog was on her side.

Fifteen years passed by since the basement episode. She never told anyone, not even Vera, about the hand kiss and the spit. She was afraid that if she tells anyone, she won't be able to retract it, and she will have to accept what had happened. Vera remains her only proof that her previous life was not a dream. They were friends and neighbors before, and Milly is imagining how their tombstones will look; Bucharest-Tel Aviv-Montreal would be written on her's and Vera's, Bucharest-Tel Aviv-Montreal-San Diego on Alex's.

The first five years after Milly's separation were a mess. She wasn't a stay-at-home mom enjoying her garden anymore, but a full-time nurse and a part-time mom sharing the kids with Alex. It was her calling to be a helper for sick people. There was the Egyptian teen born with a bone disease, the old blind Montenegro grandma, and the dying eighty-year-old Italian with Alzheimer's. She was constantly on the road. She was busy being angry, hating Alex and refusing to sign the divorce papers. Her hate was mixed with the hope that they will go back together.

While slowly getting to the bathroom, leaning against the dirty walls, moving around the house without a cane while gasping for air like a fish on shore, she remembers how she used to leave nasty messages at his workplace. Then she used to drink heavily, blaming him for everything; for stealing the kids and the dog from her, for their daughter's drug abuse, for not sending enough money even if her income was a quarter of his.

Finally she gave up and signed the divorce papers, her signature more like a deep cut in her flesh. Day and night, she saw the last page of the divorce papers, blinding her; their signatures, signatures of hate now, were the same as their signatures when they had gotten married, once signatures of love.

When Alex relocated to California and became a father again at fifty-five, she hated him even more. She felt like puking, only imagining him fornicating and asking herself how the new younger woman, the whore, was satisfying him. *Screw them!* she thought. At this time her son was still with her in Montreal and her daughter with Alex in California. Those were the good years!

But those years are gone now. Her son had finished his studies at McGill University, left on a scholarship to Chicago, and never came back as he promised. With no money left from her half of the sold family house, she had to downgrade to a basement apartment in an unkempt building in a poor neighborhood, her last station. She is still here ten years later. Her son is now a big shot, working in San Francisco and NY for a company whose name she forgets. Even if her son visits her every six months or so, he never stays long, repulsed by her place, by Stefan, or by her crying face, her puffy eyes and her snotty nose. When she sees him at the door too afraid to enter, she loses it. "Now you're too precious to even enter and smoke a joint with Stefan? What? Is Stefan below you? You're not able to spend one hour with me? You have to run to your rich friends in Westmount? I bet that they don't even know where I live now."

They both remember his last words before he left for his studies in Chicago: "I will come back, Mom, and I will buy you back our old house and a new car." But now, after every short visit, he is in a hurry to escape from her hug as if he were an orphan or a thief, leaving her off balance like a drunk in a train station. *How did we become such strangers? Why does he despise me like his father does?*

Milly knows that nobody understands her like Stefan, at least when he has his pot. He is a pest, but also a presence. Stefan is a forty-year-old French Canadian, sick with a degenerative disease. His hands have almost no grip, and he is not much of a help around the house. At least she had a previous life; he never had better. His family finds it easier to forget him. She's the one who calls the ambulance or the police when things get nasty.

Two months ago, he had a heart attack, and Milly saved him. Stefan wants to work even if his income is lower than welfare; the problem is he cannot keep a job longer than a month, usually as a helper for cleaning dishes or unloading trucks. Every time something happens at work, a comment, a gesture, a glimpse, he comes home angry, he smokes a joint, he goes to bed, and then he cannot wake up in the morning. Poof! Another job gone! And Milly has to find him another job.

Milly is tolerating him out of pity. He is now a casual roommate or more of a surrogate son or a stray dog she has to feed. He was her neighbor before being evicted from the apartment across the hall two years ago. She opened her door to him because he had nowhere to go. He was her lover for a while, both hungry for human touch, till she called the police. She knows that every time she does, he will end up in rehab, a waste of time for him, a period of hope for her. After three rehab sessions, he still smokes weed. When he has his weed, he is fine. When he doesn't, she has to buy him pot to keep him functional.

Once when he was sober, Stefan told her, "I slept with you because I was on drugs." Even then, she knew in her heart, Stefan was a good man whose life was destroyed.

After her trip to the bathroom, she is making her way to the living room where her iPad is.

When she finally makes it, she lets herself fall on the sofa. Slouching she lights up a cigarette from Jean's supply at twenty dollars a dozen, and she tries to Skype her daughter in California. Just as a test. It's too early there. Skype doesn't even open. She tries again. Maybe she isn't getting the right touch on the screen with her crooked fingers and numbed fingertips. The second time around, even if she is more focused, Skype refuses to open.

Her pain is still there, diffuse, starting at the end of her spine and going down through her right leg, the swollen knee and the toes. She can smell her own pain. Or maybe that's the smell of an unkempt woman. She is hypnotized by the screen. The Skype window is forever closed. Milly's iPad, a gift from her son, is her only connection to the outside world. Milly can see, can hear, but she cannot touch. She feels like a puppet without strings. All her strings were cut one by one. She is trapped in her old and fat body, in her dinky apartment, in a no-man's land. Suicide thoughts are flying around her head like mosquitos. Only Vera knows how many treatments Milly has tried, but the conclusion is gloomy. Milly needs an operation, but this is out of question. She's afraid. She prefers drugs.

Last night, her Skype died while she was preparing supper from the food bank supplies. Lately she is only getting cans, pasta, bread, and cookies. No salads, fruits, or cheese.

She hears Stefan screaming to cover the Radio Canada News. "I believe somebody is Skyping you."

She wants to jump. She has been waiting for a call from her daughter. Pregnant with her second kid, another grandchild Milly will never meet in person, she's due in two weeks from now. Stefan doesn't answer because her kids don't like the fact that Milly took him back in even after police issued a restrainting order. While getting close to the iPad, she sees Stefan touching the screen by accident. The call goes dead.

"What did you do? You are smoking again? Open des window if you are too lazy to go out. Omama complained again to our landlord because your pot stinks!" she yells at him.

"*J'hais les musulmans qui veulent nous dire comment vivre au Quebec,*" he answers while watching the news about Pauline Marois's hijab proposal.

"Des same Muslims are upstairs and not happy about the smell of your joint. We have to get along with them. Go outside and smoke!" She adds while thinking, "And don't touch my iPad anymore."

"*Merde,* I cannot go outside at minus thirty," Stefan complains.

"You cannot do anything for me, uh? You are such a bum. Widout me, you would be under a bridge. You should dank me! Omama is my friend, not Ibrahim. You don't know anything about Muslims or Jews. *Am trait in Israel, stiu,*" she yells in tongues, from French, English going back to Romanian. She does that when she is angry, her brain too tired to process so many languages.

Even when she is angry with him, she needs his presence, somebody to talk to, to argue with, to yell at, even if she knows that lately he is more of an annoyance than a help. She is addicted to Stefan and to the bloody electronic monster, the iPad, she hates it when, like now, the screen looks like a clown face laughing at her.

Milly is moaning while trying to stand up, thinking that it is darker than usual in the living room probably because Ibrahim's son parked his car in front of her window again, the same window where, during summers, she keeps a few red geraniums pots from the old house.

"So much for my light! Like father, like son. One is taking away my daylight, the other won't help me because I am unclean." The other day, she was trying to get her garbage bin outside, and Ibrahim was smoking in front of the main entrance. Milly was wobbling on the icy pavement, but he looked at her and said, "Sorry that I cannot help you. It is forbidden by Islam to touch a Christian or a woman." And she was both.

She tries guessing the time from the light's heaviness. A lost ray of light is taking over her living room space showing a myriad of dust particles like a miraculous universe. Milly has to wait another hour before having the courage to phone Vera for help. Now, it is too early. She feels, for a moment, as if fifteen years were deleted by a magic touch, and she just woke up in the emergency room with her stomach pumped and her kids standing over her, their eyes only pupils, their little faces asking in a mute language, "Mom? Are you okay? What happened?"

"Nothing happened, sweetie. I just made a mistake counting my painkillers," she replied to her kids, knowing she had lost face for good.

6

HOTMAIL.COM

"I love you," Costa said, not like a whisper or a secret but more like a sudden illumination. Lora felt dizzy, but she regained her composure. They were in the middle of the mall, a world with people in a hurry lacking time brushing their standing bodies, face to face, at arm's length, coffee in hand at 9:36 AM like any normal functional people of the nine-to-five generation.

"How come?" she asked, trying to guess the meaning from the expression on his face, the face of a man concentrated like a kid trying to explain an enormous absurdity.

"I love my wife, and I've realized I love you too," he said not embarrassed but relieved and suddenly serene.

They seemed functional, but they were not. Everything erupted in November, only one month ago, and now they are partners in sin and avid Hotmail users.

Only one month ago, he was lying in his bed trying to go to sleep knowing that he would wake up at 4:00 AM with a painful need to go to the bathroom. The house's noises were fading away, his son's cell, his wife preparing for her daily long bath, his dog barking in his sleep. He liked their house in Gatineau, on a small hill, like his parents' house in a tiny Moldovian village. When feeling sad, he would close his eyes and see himself on the top of the hill, a little boy with his head full of hopes and dreams. The loud and strong November wind made the windows vibrate. He was wondering if outside smells like winter. He thought "his life's winter is here too", his hair almost white, even if his body is in shape.

Lora, his soul's shadow, was away in Japan. He felt empty without her being close, and close means in Ottawa. The closest he could get to her in real life is when he can hear her laughing twenty meters away from his desk or when they have a strategic meeting together. She was closer to him only in his dreams, coming and going like a ghost.

He was longing for Lora, but this could be explained by the fact that for the last seven years or so, he had barely touched his wife who let him get close to her only occasionally as a favor or a prize. She complained every time that his lovemaking was too long and too painful, making him feel less like a husband and more like an out-of-order sperm donor.

> *From costa1958@gmail.com*

> *How are you? Are you coming for an outdoor walk?*

> *Costa*

Most of the time she didn't answer, but when she did, he is relieved.

> *From lora1955@yahoo.com*

> *For sure, let me finish my lunch.*

> *Lora*

Before she left for Japan, Costa asked her to write if she had time, and he was still waiting for her e-mail, imagining her alone in Kyoto.

> *From lora123@yahoo.com*

> *Hi, stranger, I left yesterday Tokyo after two exhausted days of negotiations with the Japonese, tough negotiators maybe because they didn't understand my English. I am in Kyoto, in a ryokan,*

not far from Kamo River hidden by willows crying trees. After Tokyo which looked as a science fiction city inhabited by an army of dwarfs dressed in black uniforms, Kyoto is a geisha land where everything is tiny and quiet. I feel as if I am walking in an upside-down realm where the streets are all pink from the cherry trees' petals, but maybe it is only because of my persistent headache. I have the strange feeling that I am looking here for something, but I don't know what. This place is reminding me of the cherry blossom German movie, a movie I am sure you didn't see. Bye now!

When Costa read her e-mail, his heart almost exploded with joy. He hinted many times, mostly joking, that he was attracted to her, but she disregarded him. He started thinking that he is invisible to women in general. In order to stay close to her, he invented the lunch walks. He even sent her a Stratan's song one night when his longing was painful, but she never reacted to this e-mail. Maybe, she was not interested in Romanian recent pop music, for she had left Romania way before him, and besides, she was a Jew from Transylvania.

From costa1958@gmail.com

Lora, I am so happy you wrote. Enjoy Kyoto!

Costa

Lora came back from Japan. As usual, she got up early in the morning. She liked to enjoy her coffee in the morning silence of her sleepy house on a sleepy street in an Ottawa suburb. She tapped lightly on her computer while her black cat curled at her feet, and before entering her password, she could see her face reflected by the dark blue of the screensaver her had husband installed. Not bad in this light, but she knows all the new lines on her face, another proof she is damaged goods. She had lost the strength of her thighs and the firmness of her breasts. She had lost the smoothness of her caramel skin, but she kept the madness of her heart, a madness revolting every November. She hated November, the month when her mother had died, but that day she was happy for no reason. Her body, which she thought old, was invaded by desire, something she had forgotten after so many years of copulation to tame the strange rage of her husband. She knew for a while that Costa had no sex at home, and she pitied him. He had confessed to her, maybe searching for answers from a woman. Lora was shocked and panicked. "How come a wife is not capable of such a sacrifice? Even if it is unpleasant, you have to do it, no? A man needs it."

Costa was her buddy at work; she was able to share with him all her sorrows, her son's rebellion, her husband's jealousy or her overload at work. He was constantly inviting her for walks to talk and to change her thoughts by telling her dull stories with a calm voice. He was a good tennis player she had heard, and he tried to convince her to start playing and taking lessons with him. She refused. Sometimes, he was strange. He had sent her once some songs by e-mail, songs she didn't even understand. Recently, he had confessed about his wife's condition. Lora felt in his empathy for his wife a grain of resentment impossible to kill. Costa's wife had something close to vaginismus, but he couldn't accept the fact that she decided to do nothing about it only refuse him intimacy.

Lora entered this slippery territory because she wanted to help, to give him hope that this stage in his couple's life would pass. Lora is a compulsive helper and open to share her experience. She confessed that she used to have a similar problem, a sort of blockage that had passed after a while. Meanwhile her husband, because of his drinking or just age, was less interested in intimacy and if he had given up on them as a couple.

Instead of fixing the problem by talking to Lora, he became even more tormented. Then two days later, Costa came to her desk and told her abruptly that he dreamt they were making love. His face was red, and his hands were trembling. He couldn't linger around to see the surprise hitting her like a bullet on the forehead.

What the hell! she screamed in her head. *I also had a dream.* She had a disturbing dream in Japan. The night after she wrote him from Kyoto, while she was sleeping in her *ryokan* room with paper walls, she dreamt that she was scooped up by someone with skin like silk. She almost jumped from her dream to the darkness of the place with the certitude that she was sleeping in Costa's arms. While struggling to escape his embrace, certain that his skin would feel this way, she realized that she was only wrapped in a silky Japanese night cover. When she woke up the next morning, his e-mail was waiting for her, and she felt as if, during the night, Costa's soul travelled through the

Internet to nest in her bed. Or maybe Costa was hiding in her head? Why? She didn't tell anybody, and now Costa was confessing about his dream. A prophecy? A spell? A venom? A curse? They were both rational people, working with money.

From that day on, she turned crazy, on the surface she played the tough friend concerned by the state of Costa's marriage, but underneath she was boiling with desire. She was even looking at prospects to find a new job and leave.

Without knowing why, two weeks later, she saw herself one morning, going straight to his desk and telling him, "I am ready to help you," afraid to mention how, but both knowing the true meaning from the intensity of their fixed gazes. She regretted it right away, but she was relieved she had not been specific. Even if she wanted to retract her offer, it was impossible because a wave of desire washed over her again from head to toe, there in full day. He was still sitting at his desk, his face red again, taken by surprise and unable to react, but she could see his clenching jaw muscles, his fists grabbing the chair underneath, and every cell of his body making the effort to understand what his brain was not able to. Was she playing with him?

She walked away like a soldier determined to win. She was angry with herself, and it was clear to her that it was supposed to be one episode, a friend helping a friend, the type of sex that their generation hated but a good enough patch for a man in need. She asked herself if she was an angel or a whore. In a way, she has sacrificed herself for years in her own bed. She was well trained to offer her body for a good cause. Or maybe this was her way to justify a desire for a married man. Who was she? A whore who wanted to convince herself she was an angel? Why was she not able to explain the desire making her toss in bed like a witch wrapped in a punishment fire? She was suffering almost like a woman giving birth in slow motion. Now, in pain, she finally got the meaning of Stratan's song that he had once sent her.

From <costa123@hotmail.ca>

Welcome to Hotmail, Lora. It is safer to have a new account, an account for love. Don't forget to always disconnect after sending an e-mail.

I was surprised when you accepted my plight and even more surprised when, two days ago, you wanted us to go to a hotel as soon as possible. Even if I imagined many times this moment and even if you said you are ready to help, I didn't know how to handle it. Somebody desired me too? I don't get it. Why now? I tried to tell you over and over the same thing before, and you ignored me.

You gave me the three pages that you wrote in Japan about me, about us, about something growing inside of you like a flower. My heart almost stopped when I saw we were synchronized. It's crazy, and I am crazy about you, the way you are as if you have a light inside of you. This, whatever it is, I don't want it to end. Never.

If you are sure that this is what you want, we can meet at Siesta Kichisipi, a motel on the north shore of the river.

The room was small but clean, practical, cheap, and kitsch. The curtains and the bedcovers had the same flowery brown pattern and reminded her of her grandmother's quilt back in the '60s. She had a strange feeling as if she levitated in time and space and she was back in her childhood village, in her grandmother's house by the lake. The motel was by the river. She was bothered by the plastic flower garlands framing the huge mirror on one side of the bed. The bed was good quality, the bedsheets white and freshly changed. The owners, a Vietnamese family, were polite and inviting even if the place was a place of sin, no name or registration required.

Her car, a small economic Honda, was parked outside, between two black American four-wheel drives. They could easily pass for a couple looking for a place to crash and make love without being interrupted by a crying baby. This assumption was backed up by her grandson's car seat in the back of her Honda.

He was tense, his body an open wound, his mind foggy, his knees trembling. He was speaking in tongues, trying in vain to embellish the moment, the place, the ugly situation.

She, on the other hand, was a quiet observer waiting for a catastrophe. Suddenly, he jolted, took her head in his palms to reassure her. He looked into her eyes and made her his prisoner, his arms like steel chains. She sighed. He panted, feeling that a part of her had almost melted.

From <lora123@hotmail.com>

I hate what I am, a cheater in a motel by the river. But maybe I was already a cheater when whirling in bed alone, longing for you. My brain refused you, but my body followed you in a trance. I am cut in half, somewhere in the heart area. After our lovemaking, I felt like a vase remodeled by a sculptor or as if a magician had put fire in my flesh. I am still feeling you, and I don't know for sure if this is desire or pain. I need your touch with hunger maybe because I never expected to feel attraction at my age. My body had a voice that screamed in my belly. I was living an out-of-brain experience, my body more alive than ever. I had no choice. I needed nothing else than the touch of your hands, huge butterfly wings. If it's only physical, will all this go away? And why I am telling you all about my feelings in unashamed words? Why am I not afraid of you? L.

From <costa123@hotmail.ca>

Darling, I longed for you for years. I liked you from the moment we met ten years ago. I was dreaming of you, but I had no choice. What choice could two married people have? Back then, I didn't know that I was not complete. Year after year, I just hoped for a miracle in my marriage. Instead, you became a regular in my dreams. I opened up to you because you are my friend and you would understand even when I was afraid you wouldn't. I kept it inside, in the beginning not understanding my reactions in your presence. The morning I came to you to tell you my dream, I was a volcano impossible to contain his lava. You saved me.

C.

From <lora123@hotmail.com>

You know, the first time I dreamt about you I was in Kyoto, right after sending you an e-mail about this city. Walking along the water canals bordered by weeping willows, I had time to think about you. I saw the abyss of your despair after years of abstinence. I knew this could turn ugly. I saw friends around me destroying their marriage because of lack of communication first and then lack of intimacy. I've seen their loneliness staying together or their painful divorces. I don't want you to become one of them.

While sleeping in this tiny Kyoto ryokan, I jumped out of a dream when I felt your silky body, I don't know why it was silky, scooping up my body. Your ghostly presence was embracing me in my sleep. When I woke up in the morning barely remembering my beautiful nightmare, I checked my e-mails. As you know such an activity is robotic, but I had to face the miracle of your e-mail, saying how happy you were getting news from me. I felt your spirit descending from my laptop and landing on my skin while I was asleep. Telepathy? Entaglement? Desire? L.

From <costa123@hotmail.ca>

I am so grateful for what you did for me, but I am asking you, why did you do it? You offered your body as a sacrifice for friendship? I want to hope it is more than that. I was trembling when we found ourselves alone in this tiny Siesta room. I checked the bedsheets to make sure they were clean enough for you. You were standing watching me, looking lost like a wild deer and acting aloof. I was so relieved when you approved of the room, expecting to be worse. I still did not believe you were worn by desire, a destructive desire, like an emergency need for oxygen.

You undressed quickly as for a medical exam in a busy cabinet or as if you were in a hurry to perform an unpleasant task. I started kissing you, and I felt you cold, distant, afraid. I was afraid too. I felt this was my chance. I cannot blow it, and I knew that I will blow it—I was too tense. I didn't do well the first time. I didn't remember how to do it anymore. I was afraid you would laugh or be ironic, but you didn't. Did you like it the second time? Did you like it the third time? I am crazy about you, the way you are. I want more of you, every cell of you, every thought you think. I want to know you, and I want you to be happy. I want to see your smile and hear your voice and your laugh.

C.

From <lora123@hotmail.com>

I was on fire, and while I was awkwardly kissing you, I heard myself moaning, cooing like a bird. I didn't know it was me moaning. My brain was frozen, my body idle, but my insides were boiling. I didn't expect such a brutal anxiety in my desire. You know, two days after Siesta, my womanhood was still reverberating as if a cord was struck between my thighs and my navel. I felt like a guitar touched by the hand of a troubadour. Am I out of my mind? When we met yesterday for coffee, the emotion on your face just washed away my determination to never get back in bed with you. Then I knew I am lost! L.

<costa123@hotmail.ca>

My love, I hope with all my heart this will last forever.

The second time around, while she was driving, he was holding her right hand and caressing it against his left cheek, his face flooded by too much blood and too many butterflies trying to escape his body. Their clothes flew from their bodies as soon as they closed the Siesta's door. They devoured one another for three hours as if they had to dive to get a taste of the treasure they found in the deepness of their soul and their flesh. In between waves of lovemaking, they told each other their stories and their new feelings.

They talked and talked, saying everything they had kept inside for decades. He was a wounded man, unveiling his soul, afraid to lose her before having enough time to really know her. She was in Wonderland, a mature woman never experiencing such a freedom of expression, such pure love and pleasure. She let go of the last sentry of her heart, letting him say the words, words that surrounded them in a protective blanket of honesty.

The day after, while taking a lunch walk together, he stopped and told her, "I need more of you, more from you. What you gave me is not enough."

"What is missing?" she replied.

He hesitated, not knowing how to say it as softly as possible, and he whispered, a whisper of a whisper, "I need more than sex. I need your tenderness."

From <lora123@hotmail.com>

I am discovering myself. I feel like you took my hand and introduced me to a place of tenderness. On our way back, you took my right hand again, kissing it from fingertips to elbow and back to fingertips. I had to drive with one hand while Cohen was murmuring from the car sound system, "Ain't no cure for love."

Yesterday, I gave you my tenderness. I covered your face in kisses in a haze. I caressed your body, and three hours didn't seem enough for our hunger.

I screamed, subdued by pleasure, and I loved it when you said, "Scream, my darling, scream!" Yesterday, you were again a magician with a wand of silk and a sculptor with a soft chisel. Nobody has loved me like you did. I whispered and I screamed for the first time in my life, "My love, my love, my love, my love . . ."

From <costa123@hotmail.ca>

You are right, my love, when yesterday you said that we are like butterflies blinded by the light. I am under a spell, the spell of your love. I am a teenager again when driving to Siesta, and I am panting only watching the sad splendor of your profile. I loved when you told me you want to know every detail of my life. I will bring pictures to show you my past, this part of me without you. Bring your pictures too. I want to see how you looked when you were younger. I regret so much we met so late in life. If we were still young, I would have liked to have four kids with you. I regret so many things, even the fact that after my accident, I have partial loss of feelings in my right hand, and I cannot feel you enough when I touch your silky thighs and curvy hips, your flat tummy, your round breasts blossoming in my hand, your neck, your cheeks, your eyebrows, your forehead, when I touch you, my love. I used to wake up at night with a hard-on and had to relieve myself in a thunder. After, I was looking at myself in the bathroom mirror, I had no solution. My wife is blind to my suffering, and I cannot ask for something that she is not able to give. I cannot hurt her. She is afraid of me as if I am her enemy. I am not a monster. I was hurt many times. After having our son, I couldn't even touch her breasts because she said, "They belong to our baby." A few months ago, one morning after a failed attempt to get intimate with her, I looked in the mirror of the bathroom asking myself, "What you gonna do, you fool? Tell me what!"

I am a proud man, but then I started praying like a child, "God, please help me! I am cornered by life. I love my wife, but I am not able to touch her. Is casual sex the answer? This is not for me. I need to love before I touch. Would buying sex help? I would be disgusted as if seeing pus. God, please, help me!" My love, you are the answer to my prayers. God sent you to me.

From <lora123@hotmail.com>

> *My love, when you are telling me your most intimate struggles,*
> *I am melting inside, and I would like to be able to fly to you, to kiss*
> *you, and come back in front of my desk.*
>
> *I love your wounded hand and your wrist's scar looking like*
> *a violet in bloom, like the sign of a prisoner, a prisoner of the sins*
> *in love, my prisoner at Siesta.*
>
> *I like your love talk, the fact that you want to know if I like*
> *it. "Do you love me? How much? Are you mine? Tell me, my love."*
> *Your words are falling on me like petals.*
>
> *I liked the fact that we are reliving our moments together in*
> *writing. Last time, I liked the way you kissed me. Like a dance,*
> *you turned my torso around your body as you drank me in. I liked*
> *the way you caressed me, first like a butterfly looking for the beauty*
> *of a random flower, and after, with the anxiety of a wolf. I liked*
> *you let me play Cohen's music even though you are not a big fan.*
> *I liked how we danced in this shady motel room on "Dance Me to*
> *the End of Love" and how you pushed me in the bed consumed by*
> *desire. I felt free. My eyes were wide open in wonder, in awe. We*
> *were face to face, making love and looking into each other eyes.*
> *For outsiders, we might look pathetic, but my heart is full, full of*
> *your essence, full of who you really are. I fully understand now the*
> *meaning of touching someone's heart. I am touching yours when*
> *you are in my arms. I never thought that a man could do this to*
> *me. I am on my knees, a pleasant feeling of complete surrender,*
> *ready to follow you, trusting you, listening to you, let you love me,*
> *ready to make all your fantasies come true, wanting to make you*
> *happy because your happiness is mine. I gave myself to you, and*
> *in exchange, I got three hours on your lips.*

Week after week, month after month, the Siesta room became their oasis, a magical territory where they loved each other in the daylight with more intensity every time like falling into an abyss of abandonment, like washing their souls in afternoons of amber light, two kids discovering their beating hearts or their fully naked bodies or both. When summer came, their embrace was flooded by the smell of their love, his perspiration, like rain in May. His ejaculation, a fountain of youth shooting from within, followed by their love dialogue, "You are beautiful! Do you feel me? Do you love me? Yes. Are you mine, all mine? Yes. Scream, baby, scream!"

He was constantly in need of her tenderness, his fears growing when he would see her in public, aloof and cold as if they were two strangers. He feared that he would hurt her from too much love.

Sometimes, after making love, he liked taking the time to describe her body, her face, what he liked the most, her curves, the butt pimples and the complexion of her skin, caramel color. Other times, he sung her old Romanian songs while glued in an embrace.

She found him gorgeous while he was in the shower with the bathroom door open, his body firm and fit with a penis never completely flaccid after hours of lovemaking leaving her dizzy, on the verge of fainting. He was handsome like a god after an act of creation while lying naked with his arms and legs spread in the bed, reminding her of Leonardo da Vinci's human body, fixing the ceiling with his green grey gaze and looking inside himself or way back into his past.

Their encounters became a habit and a celebration with Lindlt dark chocolate, raspberries from Costco and cheap champagne that changed into gold in their mouth. Their night tables looked romantic to them, a heap of entangled underwear, sandwiches, dark chocolate, some petals, and empty glasses of champagne. And winter came again.

From <costa123@hotmail.ca>

My love, love of my life, after I left you, I felt I was floating on air, levitating. I never had this feeling. I was a butterfly. I was a feather. I was a snowflake. I wanted to land on your right cheek and wait for your first tear of happiness. I can hardly wait to see you again even if for a short walk to our galley. I loved how you clinged to me and how you were caressing me while swirling around my body. Your touch feels good inside.

I love it when I see the joy on your face, and I feel your smile while my lips cover your lips. I hope the magic never goes away! I am in love!

From <lora123@hotmail.com>

My darling, I finally processed your first "I love you." The first one was in public, looking deep into my eyes. I got scared back then. You said you love your wife and you love me too. I didn't understand how, but I saw your face, and I can tell what was in your heart. We know we are not the kind of people to leave our spouses; we are ready to sacrifice anything only to keep the family together, this last cell of unity and support, maybe because of our culture, maybe because we are immigrants and our family ties are stronger. When you told me "I love you," I really understood and appreciated the greatness of your heart. You are my man, a man of principle, a man of sacrifice, a man of his word. In a twisted way, we believe we are the good ones, but it is easy to love each other because we have no past and no future. The real challenge is to love our spouses. In fact, this is the real love, loving and forgiving our spouses. Our love for each other is a coward's love, but I don't care when in your arms. I belief that by not going to bed with you I would have passed up something great. I am living moments of grace that I thought were only fairy tales for virgins or lullabies for old ladies. Love between two regular people is possible. Shared love is paradise! Are we crazy or only in love? We were prepared to fall in love and to crash into each other. I love you!

PS. Do I say it to many times? Am I boring? Am I too sweet?

<costa123@hotmail.ca>

Iubito, I want to keep your smell on my skin, to stay soaked in you. I was half a man before loving you. Please come with me to Quebec City. I want to spend a night with you. Pleeease! I want you constantly by my side. Imagine, we will spend five hours in the car talking. When I go to work, you can rest in the hotel room. I already found a nice auberge not far from a forest where we can walk hand in hand and watch the moon for the first time together. Would you? Take care, my love, and I think more about you!

PS. Not even ten thousand "I love you" are enough for me. Never too many!

<lora123@hotmail.com>

Iubitule, *I am afraid to spend a night with you. On top of it, I don't like you seeing my flaws. I snore, and in the morning, it takes me at least one hour to get my face presentable. I am full of wrinkles that you cannot see at Siesta. Let us not spoil our love with complicated plans. I like the way we are, no to-do lists, no schedule of family or friend gatherings, no shopping, no frowns, no lies, no day-to-day masks, no war, no questions about who is right or wrong, only us naked, two overly grown kids. Three hours every two weeks, three hours of love and honesty is enough. Sometimes your love is like a tsunami washing me ashore, but the beach where you leave me exhausted feels like silk for my soul. I am happy with what I have. I am walking on the street, and I am smiling to myself like a girl thinking how you found a secret place for kissing during our lunch hour, a galley full of graffiti, a good place to hide.*

Do you remember the young girl who saw us kissing leaning against the maple tree hidden and almost crumbled between three old buildings, smiled, and said, "You are cute." And you said," Love is beautiful at any age. You are not old, Lora. We have the age that our hearts feel."

What hurts more is all the time we wasted. I wasted so many years without you looking at me, the gaze of a man in love. "I love you" explodes in my mouth, and I am drinking in the sound. I feel sometimes like a volcano, sometimes like a flower, thirsty for your clear seeds and for your final scream as if you just entered paradise, lovers' delirium. My man, my love.

Many times they asked themselves if they were just some crazy old sex addicts, or just in love with love itself. They never changed their Siesta room. This was a tiny hidden place where no love died yet, where no anger could enter, only angels to be let in. They continued to make a reality of their craziest dreams, making love on Leonard Cohen's music, dancing naked, making love covered in petals as if bathing in a swamp of violets, making love like crabs, dogs, snacks, or in lotus position. She started having major orgasms as others at their age have major strokes. She even discovered that she was a fountain woman. He adored making love to her baby style, a position they discovered the first time when she, a bit scared by his devastating manhood, wanted to escape from his embrace and crawled into a foetal position.

They were one, a wheel of love, the man flowing into her through her lips, the woman flowing into him through his eyes.

The balance of love was reversed now. After each act of love, she became more fragile, crying during lovemaking or crying from nothing when alone. She was drowning in his love, moved by his simple pleasure to be with her outside, in nature, taking walks at noon or watching the river after making love. He stopped walking like a wounded man, his stride now almost snappy, full of zest. They knew that everything was in their heads, but they didn't care. They felt innocent, truthful, and clean, all sins gone. Their encounters were like showers in elixir to give them strength to go out, live, pretend, and balance their souls and their duties.

She kept his first love note on a piece of yellow stationary, and he kept, hidden in a drawer of his desk, a tiny picture of her.

They started with desire. They ended up with loyalty in love, holding each other in bed, eyelashes to eyelashes, mouth to mouth, flat stomach to stomach, sex over sex, legs entwined, thoughts flowing from their fried brains through their mouths, words interrupted and completed by their kisses.

They kept their pact to stay strong, hold two separate lives, lying in the name of their families who were not to be hurt. They knew that their years of foolishness were limited by their white hair and their wrinkles. They kept their madness, and they knew that only sickness would separate them. They had no choice because their hunger for love was older than their age. They knew that the day one of them wouldn't show up to Siesta, the other will cry by the river, knowing.

7

THE TEDDY BEARS' HOUSE

Today is Thursday, the day of the girls' get-together at Nelly's place. The monthly gathering is a big event for them. With Nelly, a sort of shaman, they allow themselves to be crazy once a month like women in menses, for menses are for most of them a thing of the past.

The meetings are more like a potluck, with Nelly providing the house on the west tip of Montreal Island, some tea, and the ambiance.

Marta looks at her husband, asking herself if the other girls preparing for Nelly's get-together have to deal with their husbands' rolling eyes when Nelly's name is mentioned. "Today you have the witches' get-together?" he asks ironically.

"Yes, we are more and more of us witches," Marta replies, keeping up with him. She made the mistake telling him stuff about Nelly and the girls even if Ilona told her not to. Ilona knows. She's practicing yoga and meditation for twenty years, and her husband still keeps putting her down. Marta hopes to have the courage one day to share with the girls her own marital struggle where condescending dismissals have become the status quo.

Even at Nelly's Marta doesn't mention it , a place where otherwise she feels free to ask stupid questions as most of the regulars are not afraid to be funny, awkward, maybe ridiculous, or just themselves, not even ashamed by their broken English like most first-generation immigrants.

Most of the time Marta is ashamed, ashamed at Nelly's to tell the story of her sometimes-abusive marriage, and ashamed at home that she's part of a support group, because Nelly's group could fit the definition. She doesn't want her son to believe she's like the young feminists on campus, going to a safe house to escape debate and reality. The men in her life believe that her friends are a bit cuckoo. Marta wants to write Nelly's story but is still debating how, for a story needs conflict, and Nelly is a conflict killer. That's why she gave up her project. Marta is still not sure where she really belongs, in her men's realm or in Nelly's territory, struggling between reality and wishful thinking, shaping her future.

Two streets away, Ella is eating standing up in her kitchen. The stock market is down today, and she cannot sit down. She has to close two fund transfers before she goes to Nelly's. Ella has been a widow for seven years now, working part-time in finances, and she never gets tired of it. She is alone, but still looking for a soul mate. By now, she knows all the mistakes she made with her late husband, and she has finally forgiven herself for. After losing a second love to cancer, she's convinced she's cursed and has stopped looking. She's cutting the pie she baked last night, and she's looking for a nice plate to bring to Nelly's.

In a modern and sparkling clean kitchen five kilometers away from Nelly's place, Cara's husband is washing the dishes. "Honey, don't forget to bring back from Nelly your EFT CD'. You always forget." Cara, who looks like a tiny Celine Dion, fidgety and overly enthusiastic, has a passion for teach EFT (emotional freedom technique) tapping. Those CDs were a gift from her husband for her birthday last year. She looks at him, and suddenly a wave of warmth invades her heart. She's happy to see him washing the dishes and thinking about her. Cara, a big boss at Air Canada, is tired after a long day at the office, but coming home to her husband is a joy every day. She phones Marta to tell her she will pick her up. This way Cara makes sure Marta won't skip the get-together.

No, Marta won't skip any get-together. On the contrary, Marta believes that being crazy with her crazy friends once a month is not enough. She started coming to Nelly's three years ago, the year of her burnout. It was the year the maple trees in front of her house started to cry in April. She hadn't noticed the nasty oily stains on her car before. One morning, while backing up from her driveway, she saw the windshield smeared with white graffiti. She realized then she must be crazy thinking that the trees were shedding tears for her late father, tears she herself was unable to shed. Her father had died the previous winter. He was the one who reads her soul. He was a quiet man, seldom speaking, in life as now in death. He was her strength.

Marta feels tired, her limbs like gelatin. She knows the feeling by now. It is a guilt she cannot discard. The sky is blue, and some white clouds are tangled in the peaks of the pines in front of her neighbors' houses. Cara arrives late, and they drive away to pick up Ella, just around the corner. At the corner of her street, Marta sees the short Italian grandpa sitting on his front bench, watching his teen grandsons playing their first basketball game of the year, while he murmurs a tarantella song.

Ella, Marta's best friend, is waiting in front of her house, a plate covered in aluminum in her hands. Her Mini Cooper parked in front reminds her of Ella's joy to choose her own car. Ella, with her explosive energy and zest for life, still fights her own demons, but who doesn't? That's the reason why the regulars need Nelly's get-together.

"Hey, baby, I just finalized my trip to the canyons with Matteo, my buddy from work," Ella says before she forgets. Ella and Marta have a pact to voice a thought before forgetting it. They are in their sixties, the decade of dementia. What can you do?

"Good for you! I am jealous. That place is on my bucket list, but my husband is not interested in going. A virtual visit is as good for him."

Ella continues her story, bubbling with energy. She talks loudly, jumping from one topic to another, but Marta knows that underneath Ella is hurt. Maybe her daughter Nadia hadn't phoned for a long time. Marta also knows that Ella is not at ease at Nelly's, but nobody is at the beginning. You need time to get used to a bunch of people—sorry, women, not debating, not in competition and acting sometimes like aboriginal tribes or a newborn cult. The sage burning, a cleanser of bad spirits, marks the beginning of their soirée and seems ridiculous to Ella, but she doesn't want to kill the fun of the believers. Marta doesn't see any difference between this ritual and the house blessing with basil and holy water performed by the Romanian priests. "We might be a cult, but we are still democratic." The stick ritual, another Native tradition, looked strange in the beginning even to Marta who sees how Ella is hiding an ironic smile while passing along the stick saying, "Now, it's your turn to talk." In time, passing the stick became kind of normal.

Who cares? The rituals are not important. What's important is everybody's needs for Nelly's Thursday get-togethers. Besides, Marta remembers how her parents became more religious at the end of their lives; maybe this is part of getting old, a way to accept approaching death.

They arrive in front of Nelly's house ten minutes later, a house with a long white porch, more of a dollhouse surrounded by huge maple trees. An oversized Jeep was parked in front. The girls, the regulars, love this house, but the Proprio Direct Sales sign in front curbs their joy. The house has been for sale for almost a year.

When Marta came here for the first time three years ago, literally dragged in by Cara, she was losing her edge, she was more of a shadow of her old self, a fighter and a doer. She was in full swing of her burnout and still on medication. She used to listen to her soul when young, but in time, she discarded its silent and annoying cry. She put up with her husband's verbal and physical abuse. She put up with her husband controlling the finances and stopping her from going to her mother's bedside in Romania because "it was too late," as he put it. She put up with her kids leaving the nest, but she collapsed when her son became a poker player, a drifter, maybe even a pothead, and her beautiful daughter announced she's a lesbo. Her father dying in her house was the last straw.

Three years ago, she was exhausted. She was unable to sleep. She had constant headaches. She was crying for nothing, and she had moments when she couldn't even breathe. She tried everything, yoga, therapy, fancy vacations. Nothing helped besides Nelly's friends, a.k.a. Louise Hay, Wayne Dyer, and Don Miguel Ruiz. They made her understand the mess in her head, the two voices competing, her ego and her witness. She learnt to see that her thoughts were like monkeys jumping in and out of the milky water of her grey brain like a huge walnut. These questions still linger: "Whose is the voice in her head? Her mother's, her father's, or her husband's?"

They ring the bell, and Nelly's voice from inside yells, "I am coming!" a sentence missing a bark, Max's bark. Max, Nelly's dog, died one month ago. Nelly had been divorced for fifteen years now, and Max was her only steady companion.

Nelly opens the doors greeting them, "Welcome, ladies! Where is Dana?" and she gives them a kiss on each cheek.

Dana is in the hospital again. She's debilitated by a reoccurring spinal cord infection, a rare immune system disease that the girls are convinced is caused by Dana's stress at work.

Marta is not of the same opinion. Dana left a lot unsaid about her soul. Nobody is totally open at Nelly's at first. They need time. Dana had multiple layers to hide her soul under, layers she refused to rip off.

They take off their coats, hang them in the closet, and give the two plates they brought to Nelly. They enter the sitting room where Julie, Sara, and Joan are already chatting. On the left side of the room, the table is ready for tea the old girls drink at the end of the night, with cute napkins, old china cups, and an elegant central flower arrangement. Before putting the house for sale, Nelly renovated it, but the warmth is still there in the girls' memories. The walls are no longer pink, but they seem pink. The two chestnut cabinets have disappeared. The pink curtains with pleats are replaced by modern blinds that they don't really see. Even the fireplace an electric one, city requirement, is now free of teddy bears, all of them being packed in a box downstairs. For the girls, nothing has really changed, but they really miss Nelly's teddy bears. She had two dozen teddy bears sitting on the floor in front of the old fireplace. For some reason, the teddy bears made anyone feel at home.

The first time Marta came here, she was taken aback listening to the girls. *Those ladies are crazy!* she thought. They were talking about numerology, synchronicity, and angels saving them from accidents. Compared to them, Cara, with her passion for EFT, was a sane person.

Nelly saw how frightened Marta was, sitting among the teddy bears on the floor, but didn't push her buttons. She let her observe. Everyone has their own story, their own journey! Marta came because she believes that you cannot dismiss something that you've never tried. Michael Crichton's autobiography *Travel* intrigued her ten years ago. During the six months following her burnout, she read a lot, but mostly about quantum physics. She knew that flesh and soul should be one, but this was only a beautiful concept she never dwelt on and she never dared share with her husband. Everybody needs food for the soul, even her, the strong one. She kept coming back to Nelly's every month for food for the soul. Many times, while reading Wayne Dyer, she discovered bits and pieces from her son's cry for help before drifting away. She felt unfit as a mother, and she came here to learn to be one again.

Tonight, there are supposed to be twelve of them. Ilona was coming straight from work. Thalia and Karen are the last ones to arrive.

Everybody finds a place to sit while chirping like cardinals in the morning. The girls are happy to be here to talk about whatever is haunting their sleep at night.

Nelly is the host and the leader, a moderator, a motivational speaker, but more of a guide. She's wise. She's sixty-five but acts forty. She's energetic and graceful, glowing with serenity and confidence. She loves dancing, dogs, nature, books, and helping people. She is among eleven women on the verge of a nervous breakdown, like a fine conductor of their weaknesses and strengths. Everybody loves Nelly!

The girls navigate around her like electrons around a nucleus in the West Island microcosmos, like bees around the beehive. Nelly has a purpose, and she knows that everyone has one. She knows that any hurdle in life is meant to be and has a meaning. Her little study room looks like a Louise Hay publishing house Montreal subsidiary. She senses a human being in distress from a mile away, and she goes right to them. In a subtle way, she engages in chit-chat—she's never in a hurry. She listens so well, making everybody open up, and before you know it, she's inviting you for tea, telling you she needs your help. She's your best friend now, and in no time, she will prepare a CD for you to listen to. Ella and Marta and Cara and Dana saw her in action at a Louise Hay conference in Toronto. In two days, she made six new friends from three cities.

Her house is a temple for teddy bears and for crazy old girls. A long line of ladies entered, stayed for a year or two, enough to get healed from illnesses of the heart, to only disappear back into their suburban jungle. The ladies are here to listen to Nelly's lectures, mottos, sayings, to look at her cards, to glimpse into her tunnel of hope.

Some outsiders would say those ladies are a bunch of witches: Cara, with the sage cleaning; Angela, who believes an angel saved her life a few years ago; Paula, the numerology expert, a real estate agent once and now a flight attendant; Thalia, the sensitive policewoman that had a burnout and sailed the Caribbean to get healed by the sea; Linda, the teacher that introduced yoga to seven-year-old kids; Maria, the nurse who put together a motivational course for overworked nurses called "Me First"; Lara, the nutritionist; Orly, the technology geek; Ana, the lobbyist for natural food; Carla, the down-to-earth Sicilian trying her best to be spiritual and not succeeding; Julie, the lady with red hair, topaz eyes, an injured back, but with a great love story under her belt; Sara, a fighter for every forest or tree still standing on Montreal Island; Nicole, the lawyer; Marta, the engineer obsessed with quantum physics and the electromagnetic fields of the brain-and-heart math, always needing a scientific explanation for human feelings; Ella, the adventurous widow; Ilona, the Reiki, yoga, and painting passionate; and Dana, the most ambitious woman on earth, two years ago a CEO, now a cripple.

Nelly never asked for anything. Whatever was discussed in the teddy bears' house was deep and personal, otherwise impossible to discuss with a spouse dismissing spirituality as a sickness or even with a good friend at a party, a place where you can talk about knee injury or back pain, but not about heartbreak. Here the ladies stop being pretenders and go to the heart of the matter.

"Ladies, it is time to start. I have some good stuff for you." She opens the evening with Wayne Dyer's sayings: "Life is understood backwardly but has to be lived forwardly. Don't judge and be grateful. Love yourself to love others." Marta likes Nelly's saying, "Retirement doesn't mean you are dead, and menopause doesn't mean intimacy is dead."

Nelly shares news from the absentees or old members. The angels lady is busy with her nine grandkids. The lady who wrote a book after her daughter's suicide is back in Australia and doing well. The youngest member, a twenty-four-year-old nurse, now in Nova Scotia, is pregnant. The two men, Ernesto and Ramon, wrote a book together and have their own venues now.

A half-hour meditation follows. Most of the girls are too lazy or too busy to meditate daily, and they are happy to do it here together. It feels good, especially now that Max is not barking anymore. Their bodies are relaxed finally and their minds are empty. The ladies are set for the best part, sharing. Two years ago, they used to bring a speaker on eating healthy or Indian spices for health, or Reiki, or optical energy healing, or angels, but the most appreciated moment of the evening was always sharing, talking about their most intimate problems, a daughter, a husband, a death, a divorce, a loss, a happy moment, a smile, a thank-you note, a compliment, or simply, a simple moment full of grace.

Nelly designates who starts sharing. Tonight, Nelly starts. Usually, her life is always good, but not tonight, Nelly has been trying to sell the house for one year now. The girls wanted it to happen for Nelly but didn't really want it to happen for them. They tried to help Nelly to sell the house. They spread the news in the entire community, and they meditated on it. Thalia even performed a ritual of cutting the cords, a ritual that Ella and Marta laughed about when they were returning home from that get-together. Even Max's death was interpreted as a sign that the house should go. They did all this because the ladies unite when somebody is down and they lift them like a teenager in a crowd at a concert. But tonight, Nelly says with a cracked voice and misty eyes, "Girls, I sold the house. I wanted to tell you before putting the sign outside.".

You can hear a silent sigh, and you can smell disappointment in the room. The ladies feel betrayed. This house was theirs too. Only Ella looks outside away, detached, the moon still visible but fading away as in a lost dream. Nelly explains, "This is hard for me. This is the house I chose after the divorce and the house that healed me, but

I cannot afford it anymore. I am sixty-five, and I am not able to work full-time even if I love my work with elderly people."

All the girls were afraid of this moment, as if the magic would stop. Ilona looks suddenly tired, her green eyes covered by lazy lashes as if bothered by too much light. She's sixty, working hard as a leader of a bunch of young engineers. She's also an amateur painter and a Reiki healer. She's been doing yoga for twenty years, every morning for at least one hour. She takes care of two boisterous grandkids with no help from her sick husband. She never stops. It is impossible to understand how she does it.

Julie is a sweetheart, a happy sixty-year-old widow since her kids, now in their forties, were only toddlers. Julie is Nelly's best friend. She sees angels everywhere helping her to find things she loses, a ring, a dress, or a seashell. Nelly's news doesn't affect her. Julie knew before everybody.

This lady, with the most beautiful topaz eyes, with short-cut red hair, living her life almost levitating and surrounded by angels, shocked Marta when she told her once that after being married very young, her love for her husband grew stronger in time. She loved him more at the end then at the beginning.

Sara, maybe fifty, slim, outspoken, and straightforward, is a fighter for the forests and the parks in the West Island. She's a teacher for handicapped kids, and her stories about retarded kids seeing angels are mind-boggling. Sara has a wonderful family, but she's too tired to take care of four old and sick parents. Nelly's news feels like a brick on her shoulders.

Joan is a newcomer, young and shy, with long chestnut hair, brown eyes, and beautiful hands. Joan is here for the second time and still a little scared. She doesn't know what to expect or to say. She's trying to find balance between the love for her very Greek husband and her feud with her mother-in-law living with them.

The regulars, Tova, Lara, and Orly, the Jewish trinity, look shaken by the news. Tova, a small, sweet, and outspoken woman with delicate ankles and strong features, is self-employed and has a lot of imagination. She's devastated by her mom's recent death. Lara, a smiley woman dressed casually and always carrying a bag full of surprises, is a nutritionist helping overweight women. She dreams of writing a book about her late mom. Orly, a Disney Arabian beauty with big and trusty eyes, olive skin, and long hair, recently divorced, is a savvy technology buff, the opposite of Julie who doesn't have a computer.

Thalia, the policewoman of Greek descent, is positive and assertive. She put on a little weight since last year. She mellowed down, but she's still loud and a bit pushy. Today, her boisterous demeanor helps the girls when she says, "We should embrace the change. Don't cross your arms to protect your heart. Open up your chest and look to the future."

This house was important to the regulars. This was the teddy bears' house. Everybody but especially Orly was moved by Nelly's story about this one huge teddy bear Nelly had wanted to give away, too big for her small house. When a neighbor's wife got sick, the huge teddy bear found a home in the sickbed of this woman.

In this house full of teddy bears, Marta realized that she used to be a teddy bear too. Marta remembered how her mom used to call her in the morning, "Wake up, my teddy bear cub!" Marta was then only four years old.

In this house on the front porch, Cara had opened up about her mom's high expectations crushing her youth and cried with Nelly, almost five years ago. Cara intervenes, "This means our energy moved destiny. What we did together worked." Every time Cara talks, it is like she is starting a fire in her heart chakra. Cara is working hard in reshaping herself, from an old self to a better self. She's not yet a natural like Nelly, but she's sweet in her effort, and she will get there. Only Marta knows how much Cara has changed!

Yes, they tried together to prove to themselves that their energy is real, but it didn't work for Dana, even if they tried to heal her from afar. Cara wants to believe that Thalia's cutting cords—another Native ritual to get free from emotional attachments—and Nelly moving her late dog's ashes from her house to the new apartment are proof. However, the girls are sitting in an awkward silence asking, *And now, what the hell will we do?*

Ella, with a smile and a shadow of a doubt, decides to talk, sharing casually, "Nothing special happened in my life, except I didn't speak for one week, an accomplishment for me. I was in Vipassana yoga retreat at Montebello." She continues with a cracked voice, watery eyelashes, and suddenly almost broken English, "You know, me and my daughter, we are not on good terms, and I tried talking to her about us. I felt ready after one week of meditation in silence, but it didn't go well. Even this time, I was unable to tell her that I love her. Why? " After a long pause, she murmurs, "I am not nurturing at all. Was I meant to be a mother?"

Nelly says," You have to insist. You have to practice in front of the mirror. The love is inside you. Force it out. It will come out one day!"

Marta used to think Nelly was out of her mind when she has suggested Marta too, two years ago, to look into the mirror every morning and tell the mirror or herself, like in a kids' story, "You are beautiful and I love you." Now Marta knows a brain needs practice to be in good shape, the shape of happiness so she adds. "Nelly is right. It took me years to shape my brain to have confidence in my son. He will never forgive me I doubted his intelligence. I feel ashamed now. I tell him every day I love him, and before saying something negative, I stop myself. Ella, you can do it too."

Marta, who is an engineer working in a huge corporation, continues, "Girls, I need your opinion. I am working with Youssef. He's an IT maintenance guy for a bunch of engineers. He is a zealot, going to the mosque every day and trying to convince every new and young Muslim employee to come with him. Youssef is a grumpy man who never smiles. My good friend and cubicle neighbor who is a non Muslim Iranian decided one day when Youssef was passing by our desks to provoke him about ISIS, asking him jokingly, 'Your friends from ISIS are crazy?'

"Youssef stopped and answered with an offended high pitch, 'ISIS fights for a clean society, not like this Canadian society where half the couples are divorced, most of the boys are dropouts and almost all girls are whores.'

"I was sitting down, almost hidden in my cubicle. Then I jumped to my feet, my gut telling me to speak up, but instead I said with a sweet a calming voice, 'Guys, pleeease, no politics at work.'

"Youssef turn to me and barked, 'You sit down. Nobody asked for your opinion.'

"I looked around. It was noon. Some colleagues were gone for lunch, and the remaining had headphones on their ears. I assessed immediately the situation. Should I complain for harassment with my only witness a non Muslim Iranian, me, a shiska married to a Jew? I just sat down as I was told to do. Girls, what was I supposed to do? What should I do?"

Lara and Orly say, almost at the same time, "It is a misunderstanding. You did the right thing." Their reaction reminds Marta of her husband who's afraid or wary to make any interpretation in fear of being judged as if a Jew had no right to criticize without being considered biased.

Nelly adds in disbelief, "How could this happen in Canada?"

Marta replies, "I was there, those were his words. I didn't dream."

Sara suggests, "Go to him and ask him what he meant."

Marta replies, "No way, he will never admit it. His reaction was spontaneous, the echo of his inner feelings. He should come and apologize to me. Maybe the right thing to do is to do nothing and forget about it, but I feel it is a trigger warning we should listen to. He was dead serious. How could this reaction still exists? What's scares me most is the fact that I am afraid to even discuss about and be judged as biased."

Ella stays silent in spite of her experience with a Muslim colleague who exploited her gullibility.

Finally, the majority opted for love. Nelly says, "Send him love. Smile at him. You will disarm him."

Marta is still torn, not paying attention to the other girls' sharing. She remains silent the rest of the night, not understanding how somebody like Youssef, who arrived here thirty years ago like her, hates a society that is so inclusive and tolerant. Marta dreamt about being free in this country, a country generous enough to adopt her. Marta even loves the fact that Quebec wants independence, and if it could be done, she's sure there wouldn't be any violence. Maybe Youssef is right about the divorce rate, but this is part of having a choice, and besides, the next generation could be different, for a society is like a living creature, changing constantly.

The tea party is almost over. It's 10:30 PM. The ladies are standing, kind of high on gratefulness, chatting around the table. This feels like the end of a fairy tale: no more teddy bears, no more Beauty-and-the-Beast-like china cups—impossible to survive a moving–, no more huge Christmas tree impossible to fit in Nelly's new apartment.

Nelly's place was a place to cleanse and recharge, like a stop for a good night's sleep when you travel long distances. This house was their motel along the highway of life where a good word and a hug could do miracles. These walls absorbed and kept the energy and the beauty of twelve crazy ladies. Surely the family moving in will be happy here.

Nobody around the table feels that they could fill Nelly's shoes. They know there is nobody like Nelly, and no place like her teddy bears' house. There, sipping Nelly's fine tea, looking at the floating violet flowers and candles in a transparent ball in the middle of the table, every woman of this imaginary hora feels like a lost teddy bear looking for a home. When everybody had gone, the moon was nowhere to be seen.

8

THE CLOSED DOOR TO THE FUTURE

I see myself in you as in a mirror of time. You are le *Bébé d'amour, pas le mien, mais presque.* You are not a striking Spanish beauty like your mother. You are more of a common girl like me. Twenty years or so from now, I won't be here anymore. Twenty years from now, you will be big enough to look for your memories. I hope I will be one of them.

I am writing to you in the room where I don't let anybody in. This is the room where my mom died and where I am alone with my angels and my demons. The door is closed. You opened it, you entered, you made a mess, and you left without knowing that you saved me a second time. You were three years old, showing your age with your three middle fingers of the right hand.

The first time you saved me was when you came into this world. It was January, and it was freezing, minus twenty-five degrees at 5:00 AM. Your mom decided to give birth, like my grandma, not in a hospital, but at home with a doula and a midwife. Your mom is a rebel against the established medical system. Be aware! You were not sure if it was the right time to be born. The womb was cozy, and you were free to suck your thumb. When nature pushed you out, you got stuck in between two worlds for five hours. It is a miracle you ended up so perfect!

When you finally made it out, your mom had the courage to call me with a weak voice, so weak it would have scared any mother. "Mom, you are a grandmother. I just gave birth. You can come. We have a daughter." I burned the tires.

When I entered the room, the scent of a new life invaded me. You were hidden under a white wool blanket. You looked like a salmon wrap, your face and your bald head almost invisible under a big nightcap. I took you in my arms to see you better, for I had no glasses on me. You were more like a porcelain geisha doll, white smeared face, elongated closed eyes, rosy cheeks. I looked at you, and I was proud that my existence made you possible. I touched your forehead with my lips. It was the softest kiss I ever gave anybody, as if I was afraid not to crack the miraculous porcelain of your fragility. I didn't expect your mom to name you after my mom.

Since you were born, I wanted to spend as much time with you as possible to compensate for the overboard feminism that ripped me off of spending time with my kids, your mom and your uncle. I learned a lot from just watching you or trying to answer your questions.

The first lesson you gave me was about resentment and forgiveness. You are our first grandchild, and by default, you are our adulated princess. The fact that you are beautiful and cute would only help our endearments. If I could walk in your shoes, all I would feel is love, hugs, kisses, and again love. You are spoiled, and by now, you strongly believe that your whole life will be the same, a world revolving around you. You will see at the first disciplinary gesture that you will start building resentment. The heaven on earth of this early age will be soon over for you the moment your parents will start having expectations, and expectations are hard to meet. Now, I understand myself and my stupid turmoils. It's just that obvious! Now I understand that we are guinea pigs of our parents' convictions.

You taught me a new kind of poetry. As I drive you around, while being a prisoner in your car seat and eating the fruits I always have on for you, you talk to me out of boredom but almost like a wise woman:

"My dad loves me." Or "The moon is following us to bed." Or "*Papi a une grosse bedaine.*" Papi is a baby who smokes. "I love butterflies. Papa loves birds, and maman loves plants." "Tell me the story about your dream, the story with dolphins."

"Mami, what do you love the most? Dolphins or Leonard Cohen?"

"I love vaccines," I replied once.

You are also my French dictionary even if French is a language I once mastered. You understand Romanian but don't want to speak the language. When I look for words coming naturally only in my mother tongue, I ask you, "How do you say *rata* in French?"

"*Canard,*" you reply, proud you can help.

When you were four years old, you promised me that you would speak Romanian when when you will grew up. "*Mon oeil!*"

When I took you to my mother's grave, something that I had never done with my own kids, you asked me, "What are we doing here?"

"We are paying a visit to my mother," I said.

"But where is she?"

"She is sleeping. Her house is underneath our feet," I simplified.

Since then, as soon as we pass a cemetery, you remind me, "Here sleeps your mom."

One day, we were in the park together, and a Muslim family arrived, the mother completely veiled in black except for her eyes. You pointed to her with your tiny finger saying, "*La madame est drole.* Why she is not showing her face?" I answered in Romanian that she doesn't want us to see her face. You insisted, "We learn emotions on faces at *garderie.* I cannot see any on hers." I didn't know what to say. I decided to let your parents explain it. I might be biased.

You taught me joy. You are gliding through life as if life is round and perfect like a crystal ball. When you want to dance, you dance. You can feel the music with your gut. We like watching *The Princess and the Frog* and when Mama Oodoo's song "It's Not What You Want, It's What You Need" is on, you take me dancing in front of the TV. We've watched this movie many times. You know I like New Orleans, jazz, and Leonard Cohen. In fact, the first song you learnt by heart is his "Le Canadien Errant," for the only music in my car is his. This song has became ours.

I will never forget, when watching together how the boy and the girl were about to kiss in another Disney movie, you said, *"Je veux être en amour moi aussi."* You were only three. I was terrified and happy at the same time.

The women in our family are tomboys. You are different. You are *coquette.* Whose genes did you inherit? Maybe my mom's whose name you are dragging with you into the future? When you came from heaven, I was kind of prepared to go there. Nobody knew when you would come, nobody knows when I will go.

I am old and out of fashion. I am not yet buying organic, but I might start for you. Your mom is pushing me gently in this direction. I bet your parents critize Papi for he is smoking and me for my unhealthy cooking. I never liked cooking. Your mom grew up on Pepsi and Oreo cookies which she now considers poison. Even fruits are not healthy enough for her if not from the Lufa Farm. Your mom considers the industrialized food chain a conspiracy, and she is into pesticide free, GMO free, everything free. Your parents are the new hippies, embracing yoga, meditation, doulas, and naturopaths.
This is why you are not vaccinated. I am afraid for you. I see you in a future without icebergs, with women whose faces are veiled, a future following a present without vaccinations, a future of cultural, religious, racial, and gender confrontation. In my time, life was simpler. Conflicts were local. Genders were only two, male and female. The systems were predictable. Now, small systems are fused into a global one whose feedback is as impossible to predict as the weather.

Your mom believes that our body can heal by itself but has became lazy because of drugs, that the gynecologist's stirrup chair is designed for the doctor, but not a woman in labour, that the epidural is administratred too easily, and that cesarian is more of a choice than a necessity, a simple and efficient solution for the health system. Your mom gave birth to you in an almost-standing position, like an African woman. Me, the old-fashioned one, I believe in doctors and science and protocols, and at best in an immersion between science and placebo, any kind of placebo.

Your parents have a smaller house than ours, a house resonating with love, where the space is well used. They live by my mom's saying, "A palace feels small if you are not organized and empty if there's no love."

You taught me that early memories are crucial and family stories have to be told as long while as the elder witnesses are still here.

When your lids are heavy as the butterfly's wings covered in pollen, you ask me, "*Mami, raconte moi une histoire de bouche,*" meaning a tale about your parents at your age. You are like your mom, not easy to put to bed. You suck your thumb like her too. You have the smile of your father. In pictures, you act like a clown like your uncle. You have a bit from everyone in the family. You are like a puzzle of old pieces mixed up in an new order, a magical order. No wonder you like puzzles so much! For Papi, you are as sweet as the first ray of sun after a Canadian winter. For me, you are like a toy found under rubble after an earthquake.

When you were only two, we used to watch *Chu Chu TV* on the computer. One night, I dreamt about my parents. They were happy likes puppies. They were driving a gold *decapotable* (my parents never owned a car) waving at me. In the morning, I realized their car was the car from *Chu Chu TV*, the program you liked.

Where are my first memories? I have many memories from the time my grandma raised me in her village. I was your age. Those memories are foggy as if the screen of my memory has few pixels: me picking up fresh eggs from my grandma's chickens, me listening to my grandma's story about how one of our neighbors stole our cow to sell the meat, me watching my grandma preparing home made soap, my eyes hurting from the bad smell, me waiting for the fresh home bread to be ready. I remember my grandma harvesting rainwater in a huge reservoir. When the reservoir was still empty after a few days of summer, she cursed the gypsies from the village, "They are useless, unable to bring the rain with their spells." She believed she was better than the gypsies. She was a good fortune reader. She read cards, coffee cups, and cereal seeds. She knew how to cast a spell, especially the spell induced by the evil eye; she would spit on her palms and on the tip of her fingers, and she would massage a sick person's wrist while murmuring a disenchantment sounding more like a lullaby. A quack remedy but it worked every time! Your mom should study placebo effect of quack remedies. She might find a scientific explanation.

I am writing in the room where my mom died twenty years ago, maybe hoping that my very first memories with her would come back to me. I am missing the witnesses for the people that could tell me if what I remember is true they are dead now. I want to go back in time before it is too late because my memory is falling apart like my grandparents' house did. There, even the rose bushes are dead Gone also is the aftertaste of grandma's rose jam when I would eat too much of it. I knew the place where the rose jam pots were hidden; in the chestnut armoir from the guest room, in the left lower drawer underneath her nicely folded clothes. She had prepared her clothes for her last party, her funeral. She was prepared to die at sixty. She passed away at eighty-six. She amused us while living with us in her late years when instead of "Good morning!" she was lamenting, "Last night I almost died." In our eyes, it was a way to get us used to the actual event. I was not there for the real event even if she made me promise.

My grandma used to tell me her secrets because she had nobody else to tell them to and with me her secrets were safe. She also made sure I learned something from her experience. "Your destiny is written on your forhead," she used to repeat. "Don't do like me, spending a life going to bed with a man I didn't love but had to accept." "Choose your husband wisely. You can do a lot with a boy, but keep him two fingers away from his target."

My first memory with my mom is a memory of pleasure. It was winter, and I was finally with my parents in Bucharest, renting a room and a kitchen. The toilet was outdoors. I was small enough to fit in a tiny bassinet. My mom was washing me in the kitchen, the warmest place in the house. It was so cold that we had to sleep in the kitchen. This bath left the memory of my mom's hands on every cell of my body, for she was washing me from head to toe, concentrating not to spill water on the floor. Her elegant hands felt like rose petals on me. I had a deep feeling of pleasure and joy. Only one man succeded to revive this feeling while making love to me. Only one man was close enough to my mother's loving touch.

The first memory with my father is one of a broken man. It was fall. We had a small garden with two trees. My father collected the dead leaves and was making a bonfire to get rid of them. He called me to show me a bee with the wings burnt, unable to fly. I don't remember the bee as much as my father's eyes, their bright and intense green, maybe from the fire, maybe from the sunset. He looked like a man that lost something, maybe his hope, a man bent by the war or maybe by the new order. I felt important as if my father had just told me a secret.

My memories multiplied with an exponential speed, losing their importance in the process. I still feel my mom's happiness when her sister found an apartment for us in a new block building, a joke compared to your house now, but a castle for me then. It was a one-bedroom apartment where we had to fit five people, my parents, me, my brother, and my grandma. Such a small space doesn't allow abundance in anything, and the government took care of it; we were not able to buy a lot of clothes or food. Our kitchen and our fridge were small. No reason to have a huge ones—they would have been empty all the time. Bananas or real coffee were *delicatessen* in Romania of the '70s and '80s, a country where the coffee at *ibric* still is a magical ritual left behind by the Turks. I remember how my mom used to plan in advance the meals for an entire week and how Sundays, her only holiday, were exhausting, for she was cooking, washing, and ironing for five people.

We used to eat the same thing over and over again, and after a while we developed a mental blockage; for my brother, it was liver, for my mom, the cauli flower, for me, Friday's fried feta, and for my father, fried potatoes.

But you, you eat blueberries all winter long! You are a fruit monster and a monkey! When you come to my place, you are like a dwarf invited to clean my past or my mess. You love fumbling in all the drawers packed with memories, dry crayons, broken geometry sets, erasers, paper clips, stickers that do not stick anymore, old business cards and in all the closets still packed with old kids' school pics, T-shirts and shorts, outdated dresses that meant a forgotten date or a silly prom.

My writing room is the room where I hide, sometimes from you. I need my space and my love letters and my dreams. You know where to find me.

My first love, your papi, threw away my love letters sent to him during our four years of separation while he was in Israel and me in Romania. I kept his, the only proof that we once loved each other like in your Disney movies with *bonhommes*, proof for us, for our kids and for you, a love story between a Jew and a common Romanian girl. You should never judge Papi because he never comes to visit you or he never plays with you. Papi has always been tired and the king of angry. He is a depressed man. He is constantly drinking. He is not with us most of the time because he is smoking. You have to know that smoking was not always a crime. He loves dogs and blues the most. Papi is not well, and he needs us. You should love your mom more because she has such a father.

Many times I wanted to leave Papi. He was not a soft father. He yelled a lot. He ripped me off of the pleasure of having our kids jumping to join us in the morning for a family hug under the covers. I always wondered if it is better, for your mom and uncle, to have an angry father always present or a happy father on the weekends. When your mom or uncle had nightmares, I was not allowed to bring them in our bed to confort them. Papi never told them bedtime stories. I am in no right to blame him. He didn't want kids. He just tolerated my craving to have them. Papi loved me, your mom, and your uncle in the only way he knew. He loves you very much. His coldness and his need for control is still a bit borderline. He was born like that, and people don't change. You have to know that life is not happiness all the time and that we live a life we don't choose.

Many men saw the sadness in my eyes and tried to convince me that they can make me happy. I loved one of them; he loved me too. He didn't care for my letters apologizing that I cannot be with him. He told me, "I need you, not your letters." He waited for me to leave Papi and split up the family. I didn't let it happen. I kept my kids and my love letters.

My last love is my writing, the perfect love, my final love, never going dry, no strings, no limits, no fake orgasms, no lies, no remorse, only freedom, Leonard Cohen, pleasure, and surrender. This was supposed to be my little secret hidden under a pen name.

But you, intrigued by the closed door, entered the room looking for me, fumbled in the closet trying to hide under my late mother's clothes and found yourself immersed in my secrets.

The joy of the truth invaded you. You opened the door. You picked up the yellowish love letters. You threw them around and started dancing and singing "Let It Go," a song from the movie *Frozen*. When your mom entered the room, the words "my love" were now in a myriad of shredded papers. Those words attacked her like locusts. I was looking at the two of you, afraid that I would lose you both. But again, everything is about perception, right?

In spite of the painful and the illicit life I had to lead to keep my soul afloat, I stayed with Papi hoping that the future will give me you, *le bébé d'amour.*

Acknowledgements

All the characters in the eight short stories are fictional and inspired by Leonard Cohen's life vision. That is why my first praise goes to him. While I was writing my last story of this book, my lord passed away, leaving behind a vacuum impossible to fill. His books and his music followed me everywhere. He was the one to show me the magic of English language, and he is the reason why I decided to start writing in English. Good-bye, my lord!

I have to thank you, Ilona Martonfi, my creative writing teacher, from all my heart for lifting my spirit when I was out of words, for pushing my buttons to open my guts and spill the tears not yet shed.

My gratitude goes to Felicia Mihali, the author of *The Darling of Kandahar.* She is an example, an ideal to emulate, and a star to follow. She is my inspiration, a Romanian writer who made it in English and in French in Quebec.

Another great and unexpected inspiration was Mircea Cărtărescu's books *Why We Love Women* and *Nostalgia.* He taught me good lessons about men, dreams, and desires. He is the greatest Romanian poet and writer of our time.

I am grateful to my family and my friends supporting me in my new endeavor, especially my good friends and my toughest critics, Adriana Serbanescu and Gabi Stefanescu.

Last but not least, my gratitude goes to Xlibris professional team for helping me to realize my dream since I was thirteen.

About the Book

The eight short stories show the life, challenges, endearments, and loss of eight women at different ages and different stages in life and of different conditions—most of them of Romanian descent and living in Israel, Canada, or USA. They are struggling with loneliness, fear, and loss of touch with today society and its rapid technological changes. All of them are longing for love and acceptance.

About the Author

Vera Oren is a sixty-year-old electrical engineer born in Bucharest to a poor family. She fell madly in love with her husband, and she left Romania for Israel in 1980, where she spent six years. She is currently living in Montreal with her husband. She has two kids. She loves writing. This book is her first book.

63501426R00066

Made in the USA
Middletown, DE
03 February 2018